THE SPRING OF OUR EXILE

ROBERT FUNDERBURK

BETHANY HOUSE PUBLISHERS

MINNEAPOLIS, MINNESOTA 55438

Published by Bethany House Publishers
A Ministry of Bethany Fellowship International
11400 Hampshire Avenue South
Minneapolis, Minnesota 55438
www.bethanyhouse.com

Printed in the United States of America by
Bethany Press International, Minneapolis, Minnesota 55438

ISBN 1–55661–617–1

For Moody Adams

In August 1957, your fast ended
When a boy of fifteen
Gave his heart to Jesus.

All that's left is a grassy spot
And one old pine.

But I'll always remember:
The little white frame church,
And the altar,
And that young evangelist
Who cried out to God
For the lost.

ROBERT FUNDERBURK is the author of THE INNOCENT YEARS series wtih Bethany House Publishers. Much of the research for this series was gained through working as a Louisiana state probation and parole officer for twenty years. He and his wife have one daughter and live in Louisiana.

CONTENTS

PART ONE

—

SUSAN

1

NIGHT CHASE

Half-asleep at the steering wheel, Dylan St. John suddenly came fully awake at the high dopplered whine of a sports car speeding past his unmarked sheriff's unit. Gripping the wheel as a torrent of gravel and shells spanged off his doors and windows, he instinctively jerked his car as far to the shoulder of the road as possible. Almost immediately, a heavy black sedan roared by in obvious pursuit of the smaller car.

Before Dylan could plug the dome light into the cigarette lighter and slap it onto the car's roof, he watched the sedan pull alongside the sports car and then slam into the driver's side, forcing it toward the narrow shoulder. The brake lights of the little car winked frantically as the driver tried to gain control, but Dylan could see that the driver was fighting a losing battle. The sports car fishtailed in the white shells at the side of the road, then with a shrieking of metal and a shower of water, it plunged into the edge of the bayou amid a tangle of reeds, cattails, and cypress knees.

The black sedan skidded in the soft ground beyond the shoulder, its door flying open before it came to a stop. A broad-shouldered man with long dark hair and wearing a tan trench coat sprinted toward the half-submerged car. In his right hand he carried a blue steel revolver. Taking no notice of the Ford

11

sedan that braked to a stop just beyond the wrecked car, he leaped down the low bank into the shallows, broke the driver's window with the gun barrel, and jerked the door open.

In the beam of his own headlights, Dylan raced toward the sports car. The man with the revolver grabbed a slender, blond woman, screaming hysterically, by the arm and began dragging her from the car, its lights still gleaming beneath the bayou's dark surface.

"Put your weapon down!" Dylan ordered, stopping forty feet from the man and the screaming woman, his feet apart, knees slightly bent. He held a Colt .45 automatic in his right hand, his detective's shield in his left.

The man in the trench coat seemed oblivious to everything except the woman. He shouted a stream of obscenities at her, then raised his pistol as if to slam the barrel against her head.

Dylan fired two shots into the ground. The thunder of the .45 shattered the night air. "Police officer! Put your weapon down!"

The man shook his head, squinting into the glare of Dylan's headlights, then he released the woman. She dropped to her knees in the tall grass at the bayou's edge.

Dylan relaxed. Suddenly, he saw the white acetylene flash at the end of the revolver's barrel, heard the roar of the discharge and the bullet whine past his ear. Two more shots zipped past before he threw himself to the ground, rolled over twice, and stopped on his stomach, arms stretched in front of him. Bringing the front sight of the automatic to bear on the man's broad chest, he fired four times as fast as he could pull the trigger.

The first shot grazed the lobe of the man's right ear, the second and third thudded into a willow trunk behind him. The fourth slug slammed into the man's chest, lifting him off the ground like a blow from a sledgehammer. He thudded against the soft ground on his back, then managed to struggle to his knees, reaching toward the distant stars with one grasping hand as though to replace the light that was flooding from his eyes. Then he pitched sideways and lay crumpled at the water's edge . . . perfectly still.

Dylan stood up slowly. Grasping his pistol with one hand, he walked over to the man and knelt next to him. No movement of the chest . . . no pulse at the jugular vein.

The woman, her delicate pastel dress muddy and soaked with swamp water, still knelt in the grass, her head down, sobbing. Her long pale hair covered her face, as though veiling her from the sudden violence that had broken in upon her life.

Shoving his pistol into its holster, Dylan approached the woman and spoke softly to her. "Are you hurt?"

The woman, cradling herself in her own arms, took no notice of his words, the sound of her weeping muted by the night wind blowing through the tall grass.

Kneeling beside her, Dylan placed his hand on her shoulder and felt her trembling beneath his touch. He could see no apparent injury, and she didn't seem to be in any physical pain. "I'm going to get some help." He took his leather jacket off and wrapped it about her shoulders, then ran back to his car.

"Patch me through to Emile's house," Dylan told the dispatcher after he had reported the shooting and requested an ambulance for the woman.

"Sure thing." The dispatcher, a college student who worked part time at night for the sheriff's office, sounded shaken. "You all right, Mr. St. John?"

"I'm fine." Dylan felt a sense of unreality setting in and had to fight to keep his thoughts focused.

Emile's voice suddenly crackled on the car's radio. "What happened out there?"

Dylan felt too confused to give a rational accounting of what had happened. "I'll tell you about it when you get here, Emile," he said in a deadpan voice. "But he didn't give me any choice." The words sounded empty to him even as he spoke them. He gazed through the windshield toward the edge of the bayou at the dark bulk that had once housed a soul and a spirit.

Getting out of the car, Dylan walked slowly on the heels of his own shadow over to the weeping woman and knelt next to her again. "The ambulance is on the way to take you to the hospital. They'll take good care of you. Is there anything I can do?"

The woman replied by taking Dylan's right hand in both of hers. She remained as she was—head down, her hair a long silken veil between her and the night.

Numbly, Dylan felt the soft touch of her trembling hands encircling his. Staring across the bayou, he listened to night winds and the haunting bellow of a bull alligator from some-where in the trackless Atchafalaya Basin.

Flashing blue lights on two sheriff's units swept the windy darkness. A tow truck's winch whined as the sports car, drip-ping and muddy, lurched from its cradle of swamp water and cypress knees. A hollow-eyed man in a rumpled business suit, his trousers tucked inside rubber boots and a cigarette tucked inside the corner of his mouth, knelt next to the lifeless body at the bayou's edge.

Dylan sat on the hood of his car, legs dangling over the fender. "Maybe the guy was on drugs or something. I can't figure it." He watched the ambulance pull away, carrying the woman.

"I expect the girl can give us some answers," Emile said. His hair was as dark as Dylan's, but curly and flecked with gray. "You want to take a statement from her at the hospital in the morning?"

Dylan watched a hearse pull into the place the ambulance had occupied along the side of the blacktop. "Yeah. I don't think she's hurt much, just shaken up—mild shock, maybe. The doctor said she'd probably be all right tomorrow." He felt as though his nerve-endings had been blunted. The world seemed to have somehow pulled back from him, leaving him slightly out of touch and his surroundings slightly out of focus.

"You have any idea why the guy tried to take you out?"

Shaking his head, Dylan answered, "Nope. He didn't even know I was there until I told him to drop the gun." Dylan closed his eyes and saw again the bright, winking light from the tall man's gun barrel. "Then he just opened up on me."

Glancing at the big sedan still parked on the side of the road, Emile said, "California plates." The words seemed to provide him with an explanation of sorts.

Dylan gazed at a photographer taking shots of the body from various angles. He felt the sudden pull of home where his wife and daughter awaited him.

"Maybe you'd better get on home," Emile said. "I didn't tell Susan what happened, but I did tell her you were going to be late. I'm sure she's wondering what's going on by now." A smile lighted his tanned face. "Erin answered the phone. She sounds so grown up now."

"Five, but she acts eighteen sometimes." Dylan smiled as he always did when he thought of his daughter, the image of her mother except for her blond hair.

"Seems like just a few days ago we were hauling Susan up to the hospital in Baton Rouge. Pouring down rain, cold . . . and all the rest. What a night that was!"

"You finished with me?"

Emile nodded. "Yep. I've got all I need. I'll write up the report tomorrow."

Sliding off the fender, Dylan got into his car. As he pulled onto the road, he took a final look at the man he had shot. The pudgy mortician in an ill-fitting black suit pulled up the zipper of the heavy plastic bag, blotting out the face that gleamed like cold, pale marble in the dim light.

Dylan drove into the tin-roofed shed that stood on a narrow strip of ground between the road and the water. Turning the key in the ignition, he breathed in the smells of damp earth and musty old timbers. The engine made ticking sounds as it cooled. An owl hooted softly in the darkness.

Through the door leading out to the water, he saw the weathered dock, silvery in the moonlight, and past it the gleaming surface of the bayou and the dark tree line on the opposite shore. An errant breeze off the water felt cold against his face.

Getting out of the car, Dylan walked beneath an aluminum bateau hanging from the ceiling joists and past a ten-horse Mercury outboard motor screwed down tightly to a two-by-four nailed to the wall. He glanced at the dark shapes of hunting and fishing gear hanging from the wall and cluttering the shelves, then stepped through the side door onto the path that led to the board-and-batten cypress cabin.

Susan, wearing jeans and a white cotton sweater, stepped onto the tin-roofed gallery that ran the length of the cabin facing the water. "I thought I heard you out here. It's so late, I was beginning to worry about you."

The sound of Susan's voice always lifted the burdens of the day. Dylan started to answer, but the words seemed to catch in his throat. He forced his lips into a half-smile and stepped up onto the gallery.

"You hungry?"

Dylan shook his head. He felt Susan's arms slip around his waist, felt her lips warm against his own. Then he gazed down at his wife; the clear green eyes and long lashes, slim nose and soft, full lips, the pale almost luminescent skin . . . all the gentle and familiar curves and turnings of her face framed by the pleasant disarray of her dark, shoulder-length hair. "I'm glad I married you."

"You'd better be," Susan responded quickly, "after all the slings and arrows of your outrageous fortune."

A question mark formed between Dylan's eyes. "I don't think that makes any sense."

"I guess it doesn't," Susan agreed. "It just kind of popped out. Maybe I've been reading too much lately." A cloud crossed over her brow. "Is something wrong? You don't look . . . well, like yourself, I guess."

"Something happened," Dylan said in a flat tone, then he turned away and stepped into the kitchen.

Susan knew better than to press the issue. Dylan would talk the trouble out in his own time, and the worse the problem was, the sooner he would usually get to it. Following him into the kitchen, she poured them both a cup of coffee and sat down across from him at the yellow Formica table.

"I killed a man tonight."

The words were spoken so softly that it somehow magnified their impact on Susan. She felt a chill deep inside her chest, causing her to shudder involuntarily. Then she saw the empty, hollow look of despair in his eyes. Climbing onto his lap, she cradled him in her arms. "Oh, Dylan! Dylan! Thank God, you're all right!"

They sat like that for a long while as the coffee grew cold in their cups. The wind chime outside on the gallery chinked and tinkled in the night breeze, and the clock above the stove plodded toward a new day.

"I'll be right back." Dylan finally eased out of his chair as Susan stood up. He kissed her on the cheek, then walked through the living room and down the hall, turning into Erin's bedroom. Sitting down quietly on the edge of her bed, he gazed down at his sleeping daughter. He brushed the silken, white-blond tendrils back from her temple with the backs of his fingertips, then took her small hand in his own.

Stuffed animals and dolls of various sizes and states of dress and undress lay scattered on the bed and about the floor. A red and yellow three-wheeler, famous for its rainy-day thrumming on the hardwood floors, stood abandoned in the corner. Storybooks with bright covers clustered in the bookcase or lay opened on the small white table with its two matching benches.

Dylan noticed a smile crinkle Erin's eyes and flicker at the corners of her mouth. Then her face resumed its serene, restful repose. *Lord, let this peace that she has now as a child stay with her always.*

———

"We always knew it might happen someday." Susan sat next to Dylan on the couch in their living room. A table lamp cast a gleaming amber reflection on the hardwood floor.

Dylan's mind had turned to his thirteen months in Vietnam. "I never really knew whether I killed anybody over there or not. It was like fighting shadows in those jungles. Even with the firefights in the open rice paddies, there was no way of knowing whether your bullet . . . was the one."

Susan listened to the sound of his voice, the words coming from a distant place in a life before she knew him. "Maybe we shouldn't be talking about this now."

Lamplight cast shadows across the hollows of Dylan's face as he continued. "Everything was so . . . remote. Sometimes it didn't even seem real . . . like I'd wake up one morning and be back home. And I think most of us tried to convince ourselves that the Vietcong were so barbaric . . . the way they treated their prisoners . . . that they deserved whatever happened to them."

Dylan saw once more the man in the trench coat struggling to his knees, his outstretched hand grasping for a hold on life; the light draining from his eyes until they were left empty and staring out beyond the distant stars. "But tonight was different." He gazed into the thick darkness outside the window. "Tonight I watched that man die."

"I'm glad it was him and not you." Susan found herself surprised at her own words. They had seemed to come unbidden from deep inside her. "I guess that's a terrible thing to say, but the thought of not having you here . . . of Erin growing up without her daddy . . . I don't know if I could bear it."

Their conversation seemed to die of its own weight, as though the words needed to speak of the night's events required too much effort to produce them any longer. Dylan felt Susan take his hand and lean against him, resting her head against the side of his shoulder. Outside the window, the porch swing creaked in protest against the February wind.

Dylan got up and turned out the lamp, then took Susan's hand and lifted her from the couch. After looking in on Erin, they got ready for bed. Stretching between the cool, sun-dried sheets, Dylan cradled Susan in his arms. Then he felt her lips pressing against his own and lost himself in her softness and warmth and in her summer-sweet fragrance as though in affirmation of his own life.

The world looked different in the morning sunlight. Dylan felt his old life coming back as he drove into town past the shady bayous, live oaks hung with Spanish moss, and the cane fields stretching flat and fallow in the thin white February sunshine. He first stopped by the office, then headed for the hospital.

Pulling into the parking lot, he found a spot beneath an ancient magnolia, got out of the dark blue Ford sedan, and crunched across the white shell surface to the front entrance. Antiseptic and pine-oil scented air washed over him as he stepped into the hospital foyer. At the front desk the bubbly young candy striper gave him Amity Medina's room number.

Dylan's boots made a hollow sound on the tiled floor as he walked down the hall and turned left. At Room 123 he knocked on the door. After a few seconds, he heard a sleep-blurred, vaguely familiar voice from inside.

"Yes. Who is it?"

"Dylan St. John. I'm with the Maurepas sheriff's office."

"Come in."

Dylan stared at the face of the woman sitting up in the bed, her back propped against a pillow. Her straight blond hair hung down to her shoulders, and her eyes were large and dark and somehow out of place in the freshly scrubbed, bright face. "Becky? Is that you, Becky?"

A sheepish smile on her face, the young woman glanced at Dylan, then stared at her hands clasped together on her lap. "What's left of me."

Dylan's mind leaped back through the years to Holy Name of Mary School in Algiers, across a mile of muddy water from New Orleans. He found himself again in that same crowded noisy hallway with a million dust particles dancing in the brilliant light streaming in through the high transom . . . and Becky's smile. And he felt once more that same sweet feeling inside his chest that made him think that life was too good to be true. "Becky Burke." He could think of nothing else to say.

Becky slowly found Dylan's blue eyes with her own dark brown ones. They stared at each other, each holding private thoughts, then laughed at the same time.

"Amity Medina?"

Becky laughed softly. "Silly, isn't it? I've been meaning to get my driver's license and all the rest changed back to my own name, but I just haven't done it yet."

"Why'd you change it in the first place? I always thought Becky Burke was a nice name."

"My agent's idea."

"Agent?"

Becky's pale cheeks flushed slightly. "I convinced myself somehow that I could be an actress." A faint cloud of sadness darkened the faraway look in her eyes. "Just another one of my lame-brained ideas."

Dylan felt the need, as he had years before when things went wrong for Becky, to try to pull her out of her emotional

20

quagmire. "Well, you're certainly pretty enough to be in the movies. That couldn't be the problem."

The shadows in her eyes lightened and disappeared. "You're sweet."

That's what she always said when we were kids. Guess some things never change. Dylan felt a slight twinge of guilt as the memories of those long-ago, innocent years rushed back, touching a part of him where Becky remained forever sixteen. "You may be the only person who's ever said that about me."

"I doubt it."

"How're you feeling?"

"The doctor says there's nothing but a few bruises and bumps. Nothing serious physically." She let her breath out slowly. "Emotionally, I guess I'm still kind of shaky, though."

"Anybody would be."

Becky smiled sweetly at him. "Dylan St. John . . . after all these years. Wouldn't it be fun if we could go back to the old days for a little while? Things were so . . . simple back then, weren't they?"

Dylan nodded in agreement. He found Becky and the memories of their growing-up years together pleasantly distracting but managed to remember why he had come to the hospital in the first place. "I guess I'd better take your statement about what happened last night."

"But after the doctor finished with me, two officers in uniform asked me about what happened. I told them that Sam had tried to kill me before, and that he'd have succeeded this time if you hadn't . . ."

Noticing the slight quaver in her voice and the fear-glazed quality of her eyes, Dylan felt he should put off the questioning until a later time. "But if you don't feel up to it . . ."

"No. It's all right."

"You're sure?"

Becky breathed in deeply and nodded.

Dylan took a black notebook and ballpoint pen from the

inside pocket of his sport coat. Flipping through the pages, he glanced at the notes he had taken from the uniformed officer's initial investigation at the office earlier that morning. "Who is," he began, "or rather, who *was* this Sam Minninnewah?"

"My husband."

Dylan found it disturbing that Becky could have married someone like the man who had tried to kill him the night before, but he tried not to let his feelings show. "You want to tell me about him?"

Becky began hesitantly. "Well . . . his name means *whirlwind* in the Cheyenne tongue," then she gave Dylan a rueful grin. "That's kind of ironic in itself." She gazed through the window at a live oak, a single cardinal glowing like a displaced ember on one of its huge spreading limbs.

"How's that?"

"It pretty well sums up our two-year marriage." Becky's words were rimed with bitterness. She took a deep breath and continued her story. "I had a small part in a movie that was filmed in the badlands of South Dakota near the Cheyenne Indian Reservation. Sam was hired as an extra."

Dylan noticed the pain-lines at the corners of Becky's eyes as she spoke. Her voice seemed laced with old sorrows and new apprehensions.

"Badlands . . . whirlwind . . . it was almost like I was being warned to stay away from him," Becky went on. "I remember thinking that a whirlwind in the badlands was nobody I wanted to get mixed up with, but . . . Anyway, after the movie was finished, he followed me back to Los Angeles . . . and"—she sounded as though she were offering an apology to Dylan rather than a statement for the police investigation—"well, he was just so persistent . . . and he had those dark, rugged good looks. . . ."

"Becky, I'm just trying to make some sense of this business so we can close out the case. You don't have to justify what you do with your life."

She nodded, staring out the window at the silver-gray moss lifting in the morning breeze. "I had gotten a legal separation out in California. Finally had to get a peace bond against him to keep him away. That didn't stop him, though. He'd break down my door, get hauled off to jail, and be right back in two or three days. So I hid out at a friend's apartment." She took a deep breath. "I thought maybe he'd decided to let the whole thing go"—she glanced at Dylan—"but he obviously hadn't."

Dylan got some specific information about her husband's family and background, then asked, "Are you going to handle the funeral arrangements?"

Becky shook her head. "No. I'll call his father. The family will want to take him back home for burial on their Cheyenne tribal lands."

"If you had to give one reason why he . . . did what he did, what would it be?"

"He's crazy," Becky said without hesitation. "He's got a brother who's a lot like him. The rest of the family seems okay, though." Then she shook her head sadly. "Seems like I've always been attracted to men with a penchant for violence . . . and vengeance." She gave Dylan an apologetic look. "Since I've been a grown woman, that is. When I was a girl, I had much better judgment."

Dylan let her reference to their high school romance pass without comment. After finishing up with a few more questions, he slipped the notebook back into his pocket and asked, "What brings you back to Louisiana, Becky?"

"My job," Becky said enigmatically, glancing at the door as though expecting someone. "Tell you what, they're going to let me out of this place in a little while. You think you could take me to my apartment up in Baton Rouge . . . as part of your official duties, of course. Then I'll bring you up to date"—she gave him a coy smile—"and maybe talk over the old days."

"Sure. I may come up with a few more questions for you about your husband."

23

2

SEEMS LIKE OLD TIMES

Heading north out of town on Highway 1, Dylan glanced at the old iron railroad bridge rusting away above the dark waters of Evangeline Bayou. "So," Dylan began, still feeling a little uncomfortable with the feelings Becky had stirred in him, "what are you doing back in South Louisiana?"

Becky had put on green hospital scrubs to replace her ruined dress. Her hair, gleaming in the morning light, was pulled back from her face and tied with a white scarf. "Well," she began cautiously, "even though I didn't have much luck with my acting, I did make a few contacts with the studios. I guess somebody felt sorry for me, because they gave me this job.

"The studio's going to make a picture down here"—she twined a few stray blond tendrils nervously between her fingers—"and I'm the front man, or woman, I guess you could say."

"You want to interpret that for me?"

Becky glanced at him, a smile flickering at the corners of her mouth. "I guess it does sound kind of insubstantial at that. Well, *this* time it means I have to find a location out in the Basin to build an Acadian-style village."

"That shouldn't be too hard."

"Especially if I could find someone who lives down here to give me a hand."

"I expect there's any number of trappers and fishermen who'd jump at the chance."

Becky shook her head slowly back and forth as she continued her approach. "No . . . no, I couldn't go back in those swamps with some stranger. It'd have to be with someone I know well. . . ." She glanced at him obliquely. "Someone I can trust. He'd have to work security at the site until the construction is finished and the crew gets here from Hollywood."

"You mean me?" Dylan wondered out loud.

"Who else?"

"Becky, I don't know the Basin nearly as well as those boys who've lived down here all their lives." Again, he felt that vague sense of uneasiness, as though he were a boy again, skipping Sunday school or gym class. "Don't worry, though. I'll find you somebody you can depend on."

"I already know I can depend on you. We grew up together, remember?" She sighed deeply. "I *do* wish you'd help me, Dylan. Everything's going so crazy in my life." She stared out the window at a row of tin-roofed shacks along a dirt road leading toward the distant levee. "I really do need somebody I can trust to help me with this job"—she let her arm rest across the back of the seat—"and it pays ten dollars an hour."

Dylan immediately thought of the two thousand dollars he still owed for Erin's stay in the neonatal intensive care unit. The hospital had been generous in allowing him to make monthly payments, but it was a constant drain on their budget. "I'd like to, Becky, but my job with the sheriff's office already keeps me pretty busy." He thought of Susan writing the last check to the hospital. "Then there's Susan and Erin. I like to spend as much time with them as I can."

Becky smiled and shook her head, then said, "Oh, Dylan! How can you refuse me? We've known each other for ages, and this little ol' job won't last but a couple of months." She let her hand rest on his upper arm. "Then you'll have the rest of your life to spend with your family."

"You always were tenacious, Becky . . . and durable. I'll give you that much. Most women would still be emotional wrecks if they'd been through what you have."

"I had a lot of practice getting tough when I was married to Sam," Becky explained, a bitter edge to her voice. "Guess just surviving him gives me a head start on *most women*," she continued, a cold light coming to her eyes. Then with a wink it was gone, and she went on in a level tone, "I really need your help, Dylan, and I'm sure the sheriff's office isn't making you rich. See, that's two good reasons for taking the job."

Dylan looked at Becky's pretty, pleading face, remembering her as a girl. "I'll do it." His words seemed to spill out almost of their own accord. He knew Susan would be disappointed at first, but the job would only last for a short time and they'd finally get out of debt. "When do I start?"

Becky threw her arms around him. "Oh, Dylan! Thank you, thank you!"

The car swerved, its tires bouncing in the ruts along the shoulder of the road and white shells banging off the under-carriage.

"Settle down, Becky!" Dylan exclaimed, hitting the brake and easing the car back onto the highway. "You'll get us both killed over this silly job."

"Don't say that!" Becky placed her hand against her throat, her face draining of blood.

"What?" Dylan gave her a puzzled look. "Hey, I was just kidding. Take it easy."

Becky quickly regained her composure. "I . . . I guess it's just what happened last night . . . and all those times before. It's really over now, isn't it?"

"Yes. It's over now, Becky."

Her expression became placid, almost as though she were a different person. "And you're really going to help me?"

"Sure."

"Because we're such old friends. . . ."

Mildly irritated at Becky's Scarlett O'Hara routine, Dylan glanced over at her. "Mainly because I need the money, Becky. You're right. This job doesn't pay very much."

A shadow crossed Becky's face. "And . . . and it doesn't have anything to do with our . . . our friendship?"

Noticing the change in her expression, Dylan recalled the two of them as fifteen-year-olds, huddled together beneath a quilt on a weathered old dock, his secret place, across the Mississippi River from New Orleans, as a curtain of rain moved down the river toward them. "Well, I guess it does at that. Old friends are the best, aren't they?"

Becky smiled sweetly and gazed at the distant spire of the Capitol building, rising beyond the bridge crossing over to Baton Rouge. "Yes, they are."

Dylan parked beneath one of the massive live oaks on the grounds of the Old Pentagon Barracks, stately brick buildings with Doric columns and galleries on the first and second floors. Built in 1822 as barracks for an army post, they became part of Louisiana State University in 1886 and served as dormitories until 1925 when the campus moved south of town. "You must have some pretty high connections to rate one of these apartments. I thought they were only used by the politicians who swing the biggest clubs in the whole state."

"The people at the tourist commission have been just great," Becky said modestly. "After all those years out in California, I'd almost forgotten what real southern hospitality was."

"You must be doing something right to rate this place," Dylan said, staring across the grounds toward the fifth side of the pentagon, which was open toward the river, then walked around the car and opened Becky's door.

"Well," Becky said, getting out of the car, "the people out in Hollywood do bring a lot of money into a state when they make their movies. I don't kid myself that it's my sparkling personality that got me these accommodations."

Dylan noticed Becky's face had gone suddenly pale. "You feel all right?"

"Just a little dizzy." Walking a little unsteadily, she let Dylan take her arm and lead her over to a stone bench beneath one of the old oaks. "Thanks. I believe all the excitement's left me a little breathless."

"You sure you don't want me to take you to the hospital? The 'Lake' is only a few minutes away."

"No, I'm fine." She patted the bench next to her. "Sit with me awhile. Then I'll go on up to the apartment."

"Okay," Dylan said with a shrug and sat down, "but I really have to be getting back."

"I know." Becky gazed out toward the river, shimmering in the winter sunshine. "I don't mean to take up too much of your time, Dylan." She gave him an oblique stare out of her soft brown eyes. "It's just that . . . that it's so good to be around somebody who's not a phony."

Dylan had no idea how to respond to Becky's statement. He felt that somehow beneath her innocuous sounding words lay a plea for something to fill an empty place in her life. For a moment, her eyes took on a haunted quality, then she was her old self again.

"Hey, I've got an idea!" Becky bubbled with good cheer. "They've stocked the place with all kinds of refreshments. Why don't you come up and we'll sample some of them."

"I don't think so." Dylan stood up. "I have to get back to Evangeline. I'll walk you to your door, though."

The brightness seemed to drain from Becky's expression. "No, that's all right. Thanks for bringing me home." She stood up and walked toward the stairway leading up to the second-floor gallery. Glancing back, she said, "Well, it's not exactly home. I don't quite know where that is right now."

Dylan watched her climb the stairs and trail her hand along the white railing on the way to her door. With her oversized hospital greens, she reminded him of a little lost orphan girl.

"Daddy, look at all the big wagons!" Erin, wearing her western outfit of boots, jeans, and fringed lavender shirt, stared wide-eyed at a dozen or more Ticonderoga wagons scattered about on the dirt floor of the Parker Coliseum, home to LSU's yearly rodeo. But this particular week it housed the wagon train crossing the country to celebrate America's bicentennial.

"I see them, sweetheart." Dylan lifted her up onto his shoulders so she could get a better look at the narrow-bed, canvas-covered wagons. "This is the kind the pioneers used to cross the country heading west."

"Do they have motors inside?"

"Not much of a country girl, are you, sugar."

"Yes, I am, too," Erin insisted from her high perch. "I'm a real cowgirl just like Dale Evans. Mama said so when she was making my new shirt."

"No, they don't have motors." Dylan grinned from down below. "Let's go over to this one, and I'll show you how they made it go without a motor."

Dylan lifted his daughter up onto the narrow seat of the wagon, then pointed to the long wooden tongue extending forward from just in front of the axles. "See these iron hitches right here? This is where they harness the horses, one on each side, and then they pull the wagon while the people ride up there where you are. Sometimes they use oxen or mules."

"It's real high up here." Erin smiled down, then she sighed deeply. "I wish we had some horses to make the wagon go. Can't you go find one, Daddy?"

"I'm afraid the people who own this wagon wouldn't appreciate that very much. They're traveling in a wagon train all across the country to celebrate the bicentennial."

"The bi . . . cen . . . What's that, Daddy?" Erin gazed bright-eyed at the people who were wandering about the coliseum and inspecting the wagons and other paraphernalia of the wagon train. "You told me that word before, but I don't know what it means."

"It means America is two hundred years old. We're celebrating our country's birthday."

"I thought only people had birthdays," Erin said, then reconsidered, "or puppies."

"Nope. Countries do, too. There's a Freedom Train traveling around the country, too. Maybe it'll come close enough so that we can go see it."

Erin's attention had already wandered. "Look, Daddy. That man has a gun!" She pointed toward the other side of the coliseum. "You better put him in jail before he shoots somebody."

Dylan glanced at a would-be gunfighter with a big white hat, a red bandanna, and a low-slung revolver on his hips. "Don't worry, sugar. It's just part of his western costume. He's not going to hurt anybody with it."

"It doesn't look like your gun, Daddy. Is it real?"

"Probably not, but if it is, he wouldn't have any bullets in it, so nobody's going to get hurt."

Erin's face grew suddenly somber. "Did you ever have to shoot anybody, Daddy?"

Dylan felt a chill around his heart, as though it had been enveloped by a cold mist. He climbed up into the wagon and took Erin into his lap. Gazing at her innocent, upturned face, he thought that her delicate features were a child-sized replica of Susan's. Her hair was the same whitish-blond color as his father's had been, but the blue eyes were his own. "I did once, Erin."

"Why?"

"Because he was trying to hurt somebody, and it was the only way I could stop him."

"Oh." Erin seemed satisfied by her father's answer. "Look, Daddy! They're selling cotton candy over there."

Amazed at his daughter's complete acceptance of his answer, her unreserved trust, Dylan kissed her in gratitude. "So they are." He kept a straight face as he said, "Too bad they're not selling it over here, then I could buy us some."

Erin turned a puzzled frown on her father. "But we could just get down and—"

Dylan's laughter stopped her in midsentence.

She gave him a playful punch on the shoulder. "Oh, you silly Daddy. You know we can go over there and get some."

Dylan put her on the seat, jumped down, and helped her out of the wagon. "Maybe we shouldn't."

The smile slipped from Erin's face. "Why not?"

"Well, remember we're supposed to meet your mother for lunch at McDonald's." Dylan ate the hamburgers out of duty, but the shining innocence of the children's faces, especially his daughter's, always made a trip to "the land of the Golden Arches" a trip of joy. "We certainly don't want to spoil our appetites for the home of culinary delights."

Erin frowned at him. "Sometimes I don't know what you're talking about, Daddy."

Dylan cleared his throat and spoke in a somber tone. "What I'm saying, dear lady, is it would be simply deplorable to rob ourselves of the essence of such a dining landmark by indulging our palates in the plebian taste of cotton candy."

Placing her hands on her hips, Erin shook her head slowly back and forth. "You're being silly again, Daddy."

"Well, let me put it to you this way, then." He ran for the cotton candy booth, calling back over his shoulder, "Last one there's a rotten egg."

"Hey, no fair," Erin yelped, running after him. "You tricked me again."

Dylan pulled the Ford into the shed, slipped the gearshift into park, and killed the engine. Staring through the door that led out onto the weathered dock and the bayou, he watched a great blue heron lift from the top of a piling and soar out across the smooth dark water. As it rose toward the tree line, the early sunlight glinted on its wings, tinting them with pale gold color.

Knuckling his bleary eyes, Dylan got out of the car and headed down the path leading to the cabin. Once inside, he closed the door quietly and gazed at Susan, asleep on the living room couch. She wore a soft, pale green robe and a pair of Dylan's heavy white cotton socks. He knelt beside her, kissing her on the cheek. As she stirred, he said, "C'mon, I'll take you to bed."

Susan stretched lazily and slowly opened her eyes. "Breakfast first."

"I'll get something later."

"Now," she said, sitting up and resting her arms on Dylan's shoulders. "You've been missing too many meals lately. I can't abide a bony husband."

Dylan felt her soft cheek against his, breathed in the sleep-warm fragrance of her hair, and felt her fingers caressing the back of his neck. " 'For whither thou goest, I will go.' "

"I'm too sleepy to play the game now, Dylan," Susan protested mildly, yawning

" 'And where thou lodgest, I will lodge.' "

"I know it, but my mind's too foggy to come up with the answer."

" 'Thy people shall be my people, and thy God my God.' "

Susan sat up straight, brushing her hair from her eyes with the backs of her fingers. "You think I don't know where it comes from, don't you?"

"That's right," Dylan laughed and continued the old, old story of King David's great-grandmother, " 'Where thou diest, will I die.' "

"The book of Ruth, chapter 1." Susan grinned smugly. "I'm not *that* sleepy."

" 'And there will I be buried,' " Dylan finished, gazing into Susan's clear green eyes. "What a Bible scholar you've become! You're just getting too good for me to stump you anymore."

Ignoring the compliment, Susan asked, "You ready for some breakfast?"

Dylan nodded and helped Susan off the couch. "C'mon, I'll help."

Together they made coffee, scrambled eggs, bacon, and toast and sat down at the table in the yellow-and-white-curtained kitchen. Through the western window, the sun sparkled on the bayou's surface, rippling in the morning breeze. The bittersweet lyrics of "What I Did for Love" drifted from the little white radio perched on the windowsill.

"No luck catching the burglar?" Susan asked, spreading butter on a piece of toast.

Dylan shook his head slowly back and forth. "This guy's sharp. I get the feeling though," he went on, adding salt and black pepper to his eggs, "that he's using some kind of formula to pick the houses he breaks into. There's a regularity to it, a pattern of sorts, almost like the lyrics of a song you can't quite remember. If I could figure it out, I'd have him."

"You mean like a riddle?"

"I don't know what I mean for sure," Dylan mused out loud. "But maybe that's it. Maybe he's come up with some kind of a riddle, and I've got to figure it out. It's almost like he's daring us, like a kid saying, 'Catch me if you can.' "

"You've got to start getting some sleep," Susan insisted. "That's what you've got to do." She peered into Dylan's eyes. "You're starting to get that haggard look . . . like when you used to drink. Maybe you ought to quit your job with those movie people."

"I'd like to, but we still have that hospital bill hanging over our heads. A few more months and we'll have enough money to pay it off." Dylan yawned, then sipped the rich, dark coffee. "Besides, it's easy work. Just checking on the construction site a couple of times a night to make sure nobody's walking off with the materials and equipment. Becky made the schedule out so I could fit it in with my regular job, and we found a good spot close to our house so it doesn't take long for me to get there."

Susan's fork stopped halfway to her mouth, a clump of scrambled eggs beginning to slide away. "This Becky Burke or Amity Medina or whatever her name is—" She frowned slightly, a tiny crease forming above the bridge of her nose. "It just occurred to me . . . she's not the same girl you used to take out to that old abandoned wharf in Algiers, your 'secret place,' is she?"

Dylan nodded, suddenly finding his plate of half-eaten breakfast fascinating as he avoided Susan's eyes. "Yeah, that's her. I *told* you we went to school together."

"So you did." Susan's voice had taken on a slight edge. "But I guess it just somehow slipped your mind to mention that she was your old girlfriend."

"Susan, that was years ago."

"And you spent all those days out in the Basin with her looking for a site for the village. . . ."

"It was only a few hours for two or three days," Dylan protested. "You should know I'd never—"

"And you should know I'd never believe you'd run around on me," Susan interrupted him, her fixed expression now lifting toward a smile. "But in all these years of living with you, I've learned to sneak up on your blind side"—laughter slipped around the corners of her lips—"just like you've done to me so many times."

"I should have seen it coming." Dylan nodded, a sheepish grin on his face. "You've learned the lesson too well, Susan. You really had me going there for a minute." He listened to her soft, musical laughter, thankful that the days were long past when her suspicions were well grounded.

Susan wiped the tears away from the corners of her eyes. "Well, I think I'm still about a dozen years behind you," she admitted, "but I'm catching up real quick." She reached across the table and took his hand. "One thing I'm not kidding about, though, is you're not getting enough rest."

Dylan nodded his agreement. "I know. Sometimes it's like I'm walking around in a fog. But just as soon as we get this 'Bicentennial Burglar'—that's how I think of him now—behind bars, I'll have time to catch up on my sleep."

3

GARDEN OF EDEN

"There's a million places to hide out in the Basin, Dylan," Emile said, taking a big bite of his po'boy, heavy with crisp fried oysters, dripping with lettuce, tomatoes, mayonnaise, and hot sauce. "But we've still got to do the best we can to find them."

Dylan sat in Paw Paw's Cafe across the red-and-white checked tablecloth from his boss. "It's the perfect place all right," he agreed. "These guys can unload the drugs in one of the dozens of bays or inlets along the coast, then bring them up through the bayous and pipeline canals in the Basin all the way to I–10. From there they can take them anywhere in the country."

"It's a real proposition, that's for sure." Emile watched Dylan take a bite of his roast beef po'boy, the rich brown gravy dripping down his chin. "Like trying to teach a redneck table manners. Mite near impossible."

Wiping his chin with a napkin, Dylan replied, "I grew up in New Orleans, remember? Most people would think that makes me a big-city boy."

"Yeah, but you came out of the Feliciana hill country. *That* makes you a redneck clear to the bone."

Dylan thought of the hill country and the sighing sound of

the wind through the tall pines and a little tin-roofed cottage deep in the woods where he had spent some of the best times of his boyhood. "Yep, I guess you're right about that." He had a sudden longing to visit the home of his grandparents, abandoned since their deaths except for his occasional visits to check on things . . . and to remember those times.

"Maybe we'll pick up some leads at the meeting in Baton Rouge next week."

Dylan frowned at his boss. "You mean that drug task force thing?"

"I can tell you're just dying to go."

"Maybe it's just me," Dylan admitted readily. "Could be we'll learn some new techniques, interdiction methods, something worthwhile from the Feds."

Emile glanced across the street at a big man in bib overalls climbing the stone steps up to the white-columned portico of the Evangeline Parish Courthouse. "Could be," he said without much conviction. "In the meantime, I guess we'll just keep maintaining our routine patrols out in the Basin. Chances of running across somebody making a drug run are slim, but we can't just give up."

"I can handle part of it on my own time."

"How's that?"

"I have to make security checks on that Cajun village site several times a week, anyway, so I'll just take a look at the area around there for drug runners."

"That's not a bad idea," Emile said. "But you're not going to have much of a chance of catching anybody in that little bateau of yours. Why don't you just keep the department's patrol boat at your place, then if you happen to run across a desperado or two, at least you'll have a chance at running them down. You'll have a radio to call for backup, too." He added more hot sauce to his po'boy. "Just keep your sights on the three or four major arteries that run through there. Never know what you might turn up."

"That's for sure."

Emile rubbed his left temple with his forefinger. "Maybe you oughta take one of the M–16s and a few clips of ammo with you, just in case. Those out-of-the-way backwaters and bayous are a bad place to be caught outgunned. You might want to take one to the firing range; make sure you still remember which end to point at the bad guys."

Dylan saw a sudden flashing image of small men in black pajamas, the muzzles of their AK–47s winking with white light, running toward him through a flooded rice paddy. He could almost feel the reassuring thumping of the M–16's stock against his shoulder. "I remember."

Emile took a long swallow of iced tea. His dark eyes taking on a flinty light, he gazed at Dylan. "You're gonna have to be real careful out there by yourself, son. When it comes to drug money, these guys mean business."

"I know that."

"You remember Ronnie Breaux?" Emile's voice carried an undertone of sorrow as he continued.

"Sure. Deputy from St. Martin Parish," Dylan answered, the images of the black-clad men flickering out in his mind. "Killed in the line of duty."

"There's more to it than that. The sheriff hushed it up to protect his family. Only a handful of people, closed-mouth people, ever knew what really happened to him. But you need to know now for your own good."

Emile let his breath out slowly. "They shackled him with a padlock and chain around his neck, nailed the chain to a cypress knee in five feet of water, then cut him on his arms, chest, back. . . ." He closed his eyes, rubbing them with thumb and forefinger. "Not enough to kill him; just enough blood loss to make him weak and to attract . . . well, you know what would come at him out in those swamps. Don't let them get close to you, Dylan."

Dylan felt a chill like a cold wind blowing through his

chest. He made up his mind then, just as he had done after his classes on Vietcong interrogation techniques in advanced infantry training, and said, "They're not going to take me, Emile."

Laying his po'boy on the heavy white plate, Emile focused on something out beyond the traffic and the courthouse and the moss-laden live oaks. "I don't know what's happening to my country, Dylan. When the law of the land says it's all right for a woman to murder her own child . . . where are we heading?" The question expected no answer. Emile continued in a sad undertone. "No wonder there's so much violence in America. . . . When we place no value on the lives of our unborn children, eventually everybody's life comes under that same bloody stain."

Dylan stared at Emile's downcast expression. He had never seen Emile so gripped by sorrow except for the one time he spoke of the loss of his son in Vietnam.

"Some time ago, it was before *Roe v. Wade*," Emile continued, choosing his words carefully, "a federal judge named Gesell said that 'a woman's liberty and right to privacy may include the right to remove an unwanted child.' *Remove*, that's how he phrased it. Sounds so much better than *kill* or *butcher* or *murder*. And he didn't even bother to back away from the word *child* . . . didn't even try to sugarcoat it with the word *fetus*.

"Anyway, at the time I thought he was insane to make a statement like that." A slow anger burned in Emile's eyes. "Now, looking back, I see that he was simply evil. To say that anyone's *liberty* or *privacy* includes the right to murder a child . . . it's . . . it's just beyond believing." He gazed again at Dylan, asking the question for which no single or simple answer existed. "What's happening to America?"

" 'Professing themselves to be wise, they became fools,' " Dylan muttered.

"What's that?"

Dylan repeated the passage, then said, "Just popped into my head."

"Sounds like it may be a Scripture for our times, though," Emile said, nodding sadly. "And another thing, did you know that the divorce rate in this country almost doubled between 1966 and 1973? We're treating marriage almost like a test drive in a new car. If it doesn't suit us, we try out another model."

"I do remember that statistic," Dylan answered. "I think I saw it on that television special 'An American Family.' "

"Gives me an idea what I might do when I retire from this job," Emile said with a wry smile. "I'll open a wedding ring business, but instead of selling I'll just lease them."

––––––––––––

Dylan eased back on the throttle of the big V–8 engine, rumbling and growling with power, as the sleek fiberglass speedboat the sheriff's office used for patrolling the Basin glided alongside the makeshift dock. As the boat bumped against old tires hanging from nylon ropes, he stood up, jumped onto the dock, and tied off the bow and stern.

The Cajun village was taking shape. Walls had been raised on several cabins as well as the general store and a little chapel, whose steeple was half-formed. Stacks of lumber, concrete blocks, and shingles gave the place that unmistakable look of a construction site, although Dylan could already picture the buildings completed and weathered fifty years by Hollywood wizardry and peopled by Cajuns garbed in the rough clothing of the eighteenth century.

From his vantage point on the dock, Dylan surveyed the site. On the far side a gasoline generator clattered away in a makeshift shed. Several sixty-watt bulbs strung on four-by-four posts bathed the area in weak, smoky light. Forming a rough oval bordering the village, giant cypress and tupelo gum towered darkly against the glittering sky. The place looked undisturbed, except for a raccoon that suddenly appeared from behind a nail keg, then scampered down the main street and disappeared into the woods.

Hearing the distant whine of an outboard, Dylan glanced to his right and saw a spotlight sweeping the darkness far down the bayou. He stepped down into the boat, picked up his M–16, tapped the bottom of the clip to make sure it was secure, then slipped the receiver back and released it, jacking a round into the chamber. Flicking the safety down to full automatic, he leaned forward and steadied his arms on the rough planking, keeping most of his body concealed behind the dock. He had unconsciously positioned himself within arm's reach of the radio's handset, although he knew that if he called for backup, they would never reach him in time.

As the boat approached, Dylan could hear the high-pitched whine of the engine, which was way too fast for this narrow bayou, especially in the dark. Keeping his eyes on the spotlight, he grabbed three extra clips from the dashboard and slipped them into the pockets of his leather jacket.

Thirty yards from the dock, the driver cut the engine to idle and drifted forward on the boat's backwash. The bright beam of light flashed across in front of Dylan, stopped, then slowly moved back toward him. He crouched lower, feeling his finger automatically tighten on the trigger.

"Dylan. . . ?"

Becky! Fear and tension slowly drained away, leaving him with a slight chill and a gigantic sense of relief. He flicked the safety all the way up, then laid the rifle and the extra clips on the seat. "How'd you know I'd be out here?"

She cut the engine, riding the slight wash toward the dock, her voice startlingly clear in the sudden silence. "I helped you make out your schedule . . . remember?"

The sleek craft bumped on the tires across the dock from Dylan. He stepped out of his boat, tying off the lines, took a wicker hamper and a red plaid blanket from Becky's outstretched arms, then helped her out.

"You're gonna get yourself killed driving that fast in the dark . . . out in these swamps," he chastened her. "Why'd you come out here, anyway?" He suddenly thought he sounded like someone interrogating a suspect.

Becky smiled at him, took a black scarf from her hair, and stuffed it into the pocket of her Russian-style wool tunic. "Now, what kind of attitude is that?"

"Sorry." He let his breath out slowly. "It's just that . . . you never know who you're going to run across out here."

"I brought you some breakfast," she said, nodding toward the hamper in his hand.

"You came all the way down from Baton Rouge at this time of night to bring me breakfast?"

"Maybe I shouldn't have . . . the way you're acting."

"You're right," Dylan admitted. "I've been up most of the night trying to run down a burglar who's making a real pest of himself in town. Guess it made me kind of grumpy."

Becky unfolded the blanket. "You're forgiven. Now help me spread this blanket, and we'll have breakfast. Maybe you'll feel more like yourself after you've eaten."

Dylan complied, then asked as Becky sat down and opened the hamper, "Why are you here so early?"

"Well," Becky began, placing china plates and silverware on the blanket, "I had to come down here, anyway, to meet with the workmen today." She squinted at her tiny gold watch in the anemic light. "They'll be here in an hour or two, so I just came early to feed you."

"That's thoughtful. Thanks." Dylan glanced at the place settings. "Real dishes?"

"Doesn't cost much more to go first class," Becky muttered, unwrapping hot biscuits and dishing out scrambled eggs and strips of bacon. "Besides, you deserve it."

Dylan had no idea what her last comment meant, but he decided to let it slide, even though it made him feel uneasy. Biting into a still-warm biscuit laden with butter, he chewed contentedly, then said, "These are great! Where'd you get them?"

Becky gave him a reproving look. "I didn't *get* them any-where. I made them . . . from scratch."

"You did?"

"Is that so surprising?" She poured coffee from a red ther-mos bottle into slender cups decorated with entwining rose-buds and trimmed in silver.

"Well, New Orleans is known for great food, but biscuits aren't one of the mainstays down there."

"My mother's from Mississippi," Becky explained, seem-ingly pleased now at the way Dylan was enjoying her cooking. "Making good biscuits *is* one of the mainstays of that culture, along with dinner on the grounds, tobacco chewing, and hav-ing a pen full of coon dogs."

Dylan grinned through his bacon and biscuit, swallowed, and said, "Well, your culinary efforts are certainly appreciated on this side of the dock."

A look of longing tempered with desire came to Becky's dark eyes. "I sure miss those times we had together down in New Orleans, Dylan."

"Simpler years, then," Dylan said cryptically.

"They sure were," Becky agreed, her breakfast now for-gotten. "All we had to worry about was making sure Father Nick didn't catch us when we skipped afternoon classes. I wonder how he's doing? Have you seen him lately?"

Dylan instantly saw the image of a black man in a khaki shirt and sun-faded blue overalls plunging his shovel into a pile of dark earth and dumping it into the rectangular-shaped hole and onto Father Nick's coffin. As the man worked to the *chunk, chunk, chunk* of the shovel's blade biting into the earth, he sang "What a Friend We Have in Jesus."

"Dylan, what's wrong?"

Glancing at Becky, he decided not to spoil her memories. Dylan told her the story of Father Nick's death, trying to protect a storekeeper from a gunman.

Eyes glistening with tears, Becky listened, then looked away, seemingly unwilling or unable to confront another loss in her life. "Remember those first days of spring?" She closed her eyes, her lips curved in an enigmatic smile. "All the flowers in their pretty pastel colors, the air smelling so sweet, the soft green clover, and"—she looked at Dylan then—"holding hands on the way home from school or walking along the levee in the warm sunshine."

"You make it sound like a fairy tale."

"Eden," Becky whispered.

"What?" Dylan swallowed coffee and carefully placed his cup on the blanket.

"Eden. I always"—Becky's brow furrowed in a quick re-considering—"well, maybe not always, but looking back now, I think of those springs as the Garden of Eden."

"Somehow, I can't quite tie them together . . . the Garden of Eden and Algiers Point."

Becky laughed softly. "The eye of the beholder," she continued in a quiet, almost reverent voice, "or maybe it's only in the eye of memory now."

Dylan nodded, thinking of those long-ago days when Becky had been a true friend to him. He thought that she would always hold a special place in his own memories because she had come into his life at a time when he needed someone to help him get through those dark days.

"You remember that morning we met at Susslin's Bakery across from the school?"

Dylan thought of sitting in a booth with Becky, gazing through the plate glass window at the khaki-and-navy-and-white clothed throng crossing the streets and milling about on the school grounds. He could almost see Mr. Susslin with his skin that looked like kneaded dough and his graying brown hair that was as heavy and greasy as his pastries were light and fluffy.

"And you bought me a cinnamon roll."

"I always was a big spender."

Becky poured the last of the coffee and began putting their breakfast dishes away. "I think those were the best times of my life."

"Even better than Hollywood?"

"If I had a way out," she sighed, "I'd take it."

"Just leave."

"Things aren't always so simple, Dylan," she said, her eyes pleading for something she could not or would not put into words. "I don't want to talk about it anymore." A stiff smile creased her face. "So, you're a father now. Can you imagine that?"

"Sometimes I can't." Dylan pictured Erin's face serene and innocent as she slept beside a fuzzy brown-and-white teddy bear. "Such a miracle!"

"And Susan . . . when did you meet her?" Becky's words seemed strained, as though more than normal effort was required to produce them.

"Right after I got out of the Marines. It was at a benefit dance for hurricane victims down in Algiers at the naval station. I was so goofy that night, I'm surprised she even spoke to me."

"Goofy . . . you?"

"Yeah. Hard to believe, huh?"

Becky laughed and her smile became real. "You must mean goofier than usual."

"I guess so. She was just so . . . pretty, to me, anyway, that I was afraid to get close to her."

"What does she look like?"

Dylan gazed at Becky. "Kind of the opposite of you."

"You mean I'm ugly," Becky said and frowned.

"No," Dylan quickly corrected her, "not at all. It's just that she has dark hair; yours is light. She has light green eyes and yours are dark. She's fair and you're tanned." He found himself picturing Susan sitting next to Becky. "You're almost like negative images of each other."

"Who's prettier?"

"So, what've you been doing out in Tinsel Town all these years, Becky?"

Becky laughed, her face becoming more relaxed. "You *have* learned a few things about women over the years, haven't you, Dylan?"

"I hope so."

"Debts."

"What?"

"You asked me what I've been doing out in Hollywood. Running up an obscene amount of debts." Becky shook her head slowly back and forth. "Some of it was my own fault. Clothes, makeup, hairdos. Going to all the right restaurants and nightclubs, even when I didn't have an escort. Trying to make the right contacts. Outrageously expensive."

"Doesn't sound like much fun."

"Beautifully understated," Becky continued, an edge of bitterness stealing into her voice. "But that was nothing compared to what happened later."

Dylan noticed the anguish in Becky's eyes, as if all the old hurts were coming back as she spoke. She seemed reluctant to go on, and he hoped their conversation would take a turn back toward a more pleasant subject.

"Sam!" There was venom in Becky's voice. She spoke the name as though it alone explained all the heartache and turmoil of her past. "If he wasn't gambling everything we had and didn't have away, it was drugs."

"Becky, you don't have to explain anything to me," Dylan said, trying to end the subject.

She continued as though he hadn't spoken. "We got in so deep that the Mob, if that's what you call them, started sending men around to collect." Tears gleamed on Becky's cheeks. She brushed them away and kept on. "Of course, he was never there when they came to the house."

"Maybe you shouldn't talk about this anymore, Becky. He's out of your life forever now."

"I'm sorry." She took a small handkerchief from her coat pocket and daubed at the tears. Putting it away, she gave Dylan a lingering look. "I've made such a mess of my life since I left home, Dylan. And it's still a mess."

"Well, it's time for a new beginning, then," Dylan suggested. "It'll take a while, but you can put it all behind you. Think of all the years you've got left."

"I think that's what worries me the most," Becky said, her words dreary and hopeless sounding. "Thinking of all those years still ahead of me."

Dylan remembered how God had brought him through the worst times of his life; a light shining in darkness. His thoughts were already forming to tell Becky about this God of new beginnings when a sudden weariness fell on him like a stone. He opened his mouth to speak, but only a yawn escaped his lips.

"Oh, this is awful!" Becky looked at her watch. "I'm keeping you from your rest. You must be exhausted."

"Kinda tired," Dylan mumbled. *I can talk to her some other time. After all, we'll be seeing each other pretty often as long as she's working down here.* "Let me help you clean up this mess."

"No, you go ahead. It'll only take a minute, and I have to wait for the crew, anyway."

Dylan stood up, staring down the narrow, tree-lined bayou toward the brightening east. The last trace of purple night vanished, leaving a sky glowing with hues of pink and orange slowly turning to gold. He stretched, yawned again, then watched Becky putting the remnants of their breakfast away. "It was good of you to bring all that food out. I sure did enjoy those biscuits."

Becky closed the hamper, folded the blanket, and stood up. Walking over next to Dylan, she whispered, "My pleasure." Her upturned face was close to his, her lips parted slightly.

"Sure." Dylan turned and leaped down into the boat. "Thanks again." He turned the key in the ignition switch, feeling the rumbling power of the motor. Backing out into the bayou, he thrust the gearshift and throttle forward. The nimble craft leaped across the smooth surface ahead of its churning, white wake. Glancing at Becky, he saw her shout something at him, but her words were lost in the roar of the engine.

4

PIECES OF SKY

"Well, what'd you think of the meeting?"

Dylan gazed at the azaleas, brightening the lawn in shades of pink and purple and lavender. "First time I've ever been in the Governor's Mansion."

Emile loosened his red tie, slipped it off his collar, and tucked it inside the pocket of his gray tweed jacket. "That's all you've got to say? What about all those figures they threw at us?"

"Lunch wasn't bad," Dylan muttered, squinting in the early afternoon sunshine. "The shrimp Creole wasn't nearly as good as Emmaline's," he added, "but nobody's is."

"The governor hired a chef from Brennan's down in New Orleans. My wife'll be happy to know that her cooking is better than his—according to you, that is."

"He kept us awake, which is more than you can expect out of most political speeches."

Emile turned toward the lake at the rear of the huge Greek Revival-style home, patterned after the classic Oak Alley plantation. "He's the best at one-liners. I think that's the real reason people voted for him. He's a good entertainer."

"You think the Feds are really going to send some agents to help us out if we request it?"

"Maybe," Emile said, gazing across the sun-sparkled surface of the lake. "Probably be too late to do any good by the time we get through all the red tape."

As Dylan passed by the tennis court, he remembered a spring day years before when he had won the finals in the governor's charity tennis tournament. "One good thing might have come out of the meeting," he ventured. "Getting help from the state police. According to the commander, all it takes is a phone call and somebody will be on the way."

Emile sat down on a stone bench in a shady spot. "You're right. Those boys probably know as much about the drug traffic in this area as anybody."

"Maybe we'll get some leads about the routes they're traveling out in the Basin."

Emile glanced at Dylan, sunlight brightening the gray sprinkles in his dark hair. "You're starting to age, partner. Your temples are turning white."

"Nah." Dylan yawned and sat down. "I have that gray put in on purpose. Makes me look distinguished."

"You need to cut down on your hours and start getting a little sleep."

Rubbing his eyes, Dylan asked, "It's not affecting my work, is it? I mean, you think I'm still handling the job all right."

"No, it's not that at all," Emile assured him, "but you oughta be spending more time with your family. Kids are only kids once, then it's too late to do anything about it. Don't you want to have all those beautiful memories to look back on when you get old and senile like me?"

"Another six months or so, then we'll be caught up on the bills."

"I know Erin's hospital stay hit y'all pretty hard. Why don't you let me give you the money now so you can take care of it? Pay me when your oil well comes in."

Dylan grinned, grateful for Emile's offer. "No thanks. This is something I've got to do myself. My daddy always told me

52

a man just ain't a man if he don't take care of his own family."

"I can't argue with that kind of advice." Emile rested the heels of his hands on the bench's edge, staring out across the lake toward the river. "How's the job with those movie people coming along, anyway?"

"Not much to it. I just go out there and check the site several times a week. Make sure nobody's walking off with the building materials and tools."

"Sounds pretty easy."

"Just putting in the time mainly. They never leave anything very valuable out there."

"You knew that girl back in high school." Emile phrased it in the form of a statement.

"Yeah."

"An old girlfriend."

"Who've you been talking to?"

Emile grinned smugly at Dylan. "Just one of my visions in the night season."

"She's just an old friend who needed some help, Emile," Dylan protested against the non-accusation. "You know I'm not interested in her."

"I didn't say you were." Emile rubbed his chin between thumb and forefinger. "It's just that California sometimes does strange things to people."

"Well, you just set your mind at ease."

Emile nodded, turning his gaze back toward the lake and the mirrored clouds now in its surface. "What a perfect day! March is a good month down here. Enough of winter left to keep things cool, and enough of springtime to warm my old bones."

"You talk like you're on your last legs."

"I think I am," Emile said. The sound of his words seemed to house contentment and peace. "As far as law enforcement is concerned, anyway."

"You're not thinking of retiring?"

"For a long time now. I've been in this business for over thirty years."

"But . . ." Dylan felt a sudden sense of disappointment freighted with loss. "There's nobody to take your place."

"I'm not indispensable, Dylan. Nobody is."

Dylan realized that he had thought of Emile as someone who would always be there; that rock-solid presence he could always turn to when the problems of the job came too hard against him, someone who had the answers in the times when there seemed none. He could think of nothing to say but "What happens if my new boss doesn't want to keep me?"

"Simple," Emile said as though Dylan's concern was of no consequence to him. "They'll vote you out of office."

"Who?"

"The voters."

It jarred Dylan when he realized what Emile was talking about. "But I can't—"

"Sure you can."

"There're men who've been with the department a lot longer than I have."

"And not one of them wants the job."

"How do you know?"

"Another vision," Emile said, pushing the question aside. Then he spoke in a level voice, "They're good men: all of them. But none of them has any education to speak of, and"—he grinned—"I think any of them would quit the job if they couldn't get enough time off during hunting season."

"I don't know . . ."

"Look, the men like you. The people of Evangeline like you." He spoke as though the deal had already gone down. "And I'm going to endorse you. You're a shoo-in the first time. After that, well, then it's up to you."

Dylan couldn't see himself handling that kind of responsibility and power. "Sheriff . . . me?"

"Look, I'm not going anywhere. If you have a problem, I'm five minutes from the office."

"That's right, isn't it." Dylan had somehow thought of Emile's retirement as the end of . . . of what he couldn't find the words for, but their friendship would go on. This simple and sudden revelation gave him an enormous sense of relief. "It's not like you're taking off for places unknown."

"You figured that out all by yourself?"

Then Dylan seemed to see bits and pieces of his life sliding together like some kind of cosmic jigsaw puzzle. He realized that he had thought of losing Emile as a boss and friend in the same context as the sudden loss of his father when he was thirteen. Though he had no understanding of why, a new confidence was born of this revelation. "I'll do it."

"You will?"

"Sure. Why not?"

"Well, that was certainly easier than I'd expected," Emile said, surprise lifting the contours of his face. "Usually it takes me a while to talk some sense into you."

"Maybe all those years of talking to me are paying off."

"Could be."

"Sorry I haven't been down to see you in such a long time," Dylan said, sitting in a wrought-iron chair on the brick patio behind his mother's house.

Helen St. John, wearing a blue cotton housedress, a white sweater, and a contented smile, sipped her coffee and set the cup on the glass-topped table. "Children grow up and have their own lives, Dylan. Your own family comes first now."

Dylan took his mother's hand and squeezed it, then let it go and leaned back in his chair. He listened to the palm fronds brushing against the stone wall, the wail of the tugboats out on the river, and the neighbors talking in backyards and on stoops, sounding as though they would feel more at home in Brooklyn than the deep South. He watched the last pool of yellow light slip into shadow as the sun vanished behind the old, tall slate-roofed houses.

"I'm glad you could get away," Helen said.

"I always love coming down here." Dylan stared at his father's scuffed brown work shoes on the porch next to the back door. He knew his mother periodically cleaned them and had threatened to throw them out many times, but had always placed them back where her husband had left them more than twenty years before. "I feel almost like I'm thirteen again, and I have to go inside and do my homework for Father Nick's math class in the morning."

"How did your meeting go today?"

"Kind of a drudgery, but I guess it's a necessary one. We had to cover the new 'Controlled Dangerous Substances' list." He gave his mother a rueful smile. "It amazes me the things people can find to get high on. They've just about taken the owner of the local hardware store and made a drug pusher out of him."

"Well, it gave us a chance to be together."

"Yep. Since we didn't get finished, I'd have had to stay in a hotel, anyway. It saves the department money and gives me a lot better supper."

"You say the nicest things."

Dylan laughed and said, "I guess it did sound kind of cold at that. But you know I've always had a habit of putting my foot in my mouth. Besides, what man could resist spending an evening with the prettiest girl in New Orleans."

"You're forgiven." Helen smiled. "Now, when am I going to see my grandbaby?"

"Don't make the mistake of calling her a baby anymore. Since she turned five, she considers *baby* a bad word."

"She's so precious, Dylan," Helen murmured, the light in her sometimes sad eyes going even softer at the mention of her granddaughter. "You're a fortunate man."

"Don't I know it."

"Things going well with your job?"

"Yep. When you work for a man like Emile, it kind of takes the sting out of the bad days."

"He's been a good friend to you, Dylan." Helen's eyes took on a remote look. "It's almost like he came along to fill in for Noah after all those years you spent without a father."

Dylan nodded, thinking that he would give almost anything to be able to sit here on the patio, where he and his family had shared so many quiet, peaceful times, and have a talk with Noah St. John. The longing to hear the sound of his father's voice, to feel that work-hardened hand giving him a reassuring pat on the shoulder, suddenly seemed almost unbearable.

Then he remembered that early Saturday morning when he had crept downstairs and seen his father seated before his open Bible at the kitchen table. In the glow from the stove light, his hands lay on the Bible and his head was bowed. Dylan could see once more the radiant, peaceful smile that came to his father's face, not as though something was funny, but the one that was always there when he told Helen how much he loved her.

Dylan knew then for an absolute certainty in that ordinary moment of remembering his father that someday he would see him again.

"Dylan, are you all right?"

"Huh? Oh sure." He rubbed his eyes with the tips of his fingers. "Emile's going to retire."

"But he's still a young man."

"He's fifty-six, and he's been in law enforcement more than thirty years. Says it's time for him to hang it up."

A slight frown troubled Helen's brow. "Will you stay on with the sheriff's office?"

"He wants me to run for sheriff."

"Truly?" Her face brightened. "My goodness, that's an important job. Will you do it?"

"I told him I would. I've tried to avoid politics all my life, but it looks like it's finally caught up with me." Noticing his mother shiver in the deepening chill of dusk, Dylan took off his jacket and draped it over her shoulders. "Emile's convinced that I'm the right man for the job, so I'm standing on his decision more than anything else."

"My son, a sheriff. Imagine that!"

"It's just a little country parish, Mama. Don't get any grandiose ideas about it."

Helen smiled and stood up. "I'll think of my son however I please to, if you don't mind. Now, are you ready for supper?"

"Have I ever not been?"

As they walked toward the back porch, she glanced down at her husband's shoes and asked, "What time are you leaving in the morning, and what do you want for breakfast?"

Dylan opened the screen door and followed his mother into the kitchen. "Don't bother. I'll just pick something up on the way." From the river of memories that had been flooding his mind as they always did when he returned to his old neighborhood, he plucked one out. "Does Mr. Susslin still run the bakery across from the school?"

"He surely does. Why?"

"I thought it might be fun to stop by there. I haven't seen him in years. Besides, I'll bet he still makes the best apple fritters in the state."

"Dylan St. John. I thought one of them low-life convicts woulda shot you by now." Mr. Susslin, his flour-dusted apron tight around his baked-goods girth and his hair slicked back tight against his round skull, grabbed a thick white mug from the counter and filled it with steaming coffee from a huge silver urn.

"One or two tried." Dylan grinned, the sight and sound of the big baker making him feel as though he should be wearing his khaki school uniform instead of a business suit. "But they were rotten shots, Mr. Susslin."

Susslin slapped the mug down on the counter in front of Dylan. "Your mama keeps me up-to-date on you when she stops in. Says you got a little girl. She's what . . . three or four years old now?"

"Five."

"So what else is new?"

"Same ol' thing. Living out on the bayou, chasin' bad guys." Dylan dumped sugar into his coffee and stirred it. "What's happening with you?"

"Same thing I been doin' for twenty-seven years now. Guess I'll always be an ol' coffee and doughnut man." Susslin glanced around the bakery, loud with teenagers jabbering and stuffing themselves with pastries. "The kids don't change much from year to year. They're just as bad"—he smiled—"and as good as when you went to school here."

"I'm glad some things don't change."

Shaking his head, Susslin's smile slipped away. "That's not quite true. There's the . . . drugs now. We never had nothin' like that when you were in school here."

Dylan dealt with that subject enough in his job and steered the conversation in another direction. "How's your family doing?"

"They're all just—well, I'll be . . ." Staring beyond Dylan, Susslin's eyes widened in surprise. "Both of y'all in the same day."

Dylan spun around on his stool just in time to see Becky Burke, wearing a navy skirt, white blouse, and wide smile, push the glass door open and walk into the bakery.

"Dylan!" She rushed over and gave him a quick hug and a surprised look. "Whatever are you doing down here?"

"Apple fritters. What else?"

"What else?" she repeated, then reached across the counter, placing her hands on Susslin's shoulders, and kissed him on the cheek. "It's so good to see you!"

A little flustered by her burst of affection, he mumbled, "Uh, you, too, Becky." He gave her an appraising look. "My, my . . . you've certainly turned into a pretty young woman."

"Not so young anymore, I'm afraid."

Beneath all the bubbling conversation and fond reunion, Dylan thought he could almost see something lurking just out of the light, but he brushed the feeling aside. Still, the question came out. "Why'd you come here, Becky?"

A look of disappointment saddened her eyes, then it vanished. "Why, to see my mother, of course. She's in a nursing home down here."

Dylan felt embarrassed. "Of course."

Becky seemed barely affected by Dylan's breach of etiquette. "I'm just dying for one of your scrumptious cinnamon rolls, Mr. Susslin," she trilled in her best southern belle accent. "They're simply the best ever!"

Susslin had been won over. "Well, since you put it that way," he said with a wide grin, "and since you were such a good customer all those years ago, it's on the house. Yours, too, Dylan."

"I couldn't let—"

"Too late, I've made up my mind." Susslin grabbed the pastries from the display case, dumping them on heavy white saucers, and set them on the counter. "Here you go."

"It's just like we were in school again, Dylan." Becky hooked her arm inside his.

"Well, not exactly," Dylan muttered. "I was just going to take mine with me and—"

"No such thing!" Susslin cut him off. "Having you two in here again . . . well, it's just like ol' times. Not many of the kids come around once they get out of school. Besides, you two were always my favorites."

"No foolin'," Becky cooed.

"That's a fact. I can still see y'all right now, sitting over by the window before school in the morning—the cheerleader and the basketball star." Susslin scratched his temple with a floured forefinger. "You did play basketball, didn't you?"

"A little."

"But his real sport was tennis," Becky added. "He won the city championship and got a scholarship to LSU."

"Well, tennis . . ." Susslin muttered. "I never was much for tennis. Kind of a sissy sport, if you ask me. But I do remember now," he continued, the energy back in his voice, "you played a pretty good game of round ball. I saw a few of the games back then. Yep, you done all right."

"Thanks."

"Here." Susslin drew a glass of foaming cold milk from the dispenser and set it on the counter. "Y'all go have your breakfast. I see your ol' table's vacant."

"Oh, could we, Dylan?"

"Uh, okay. . . . I guess I've got a few minutes."

After they were seated, the years seemed to fall away for Dylan. Looking at Becky's smile and big dark eyes in her bright face, he could almost believe they were both kids again. Then he gazed through the glass at the young faces and the quick energetic bodies of the true kids, twenty years his junior, and his own years came clambering back.

"Isn't this fun!"

Dylan looked over at her animated expression. "Becky, you're laying it on kind of thick, aren't you?"

She blushed slightly. "I guess I am at that. Mr. Susslin liked it, though."

"Yes, he did." Dylan sipped his coffee, then took a big bite of his warm, spicy apple fritter. It was even better than he remembered—chewy and flaky and buttery rich.

Becky nibbled on her cinnamon roll. "I'm sorry, Dylan. I guess I try sometimes to make up for being a failure as an actress. But," she added quickly, "I really am happy about being here at the old bakery and with you."

Dylan looked into her sincere face and believed her. "It is kind of nice."

"They were the best years of my life." A single tear left a glistening trail down her cheek. "I wish I could go back to those times and never have to get any older." She brushed at her cheek, then gazed into Dylan's eyes. "Your eyes are so blue. Like shiny pieces of sky."

"Becky . . ."—Dylan felt his face growing warm—"maybe this wasn't such a good idea."

Becky held his gaze. "I wish you still loved me, Dylan." Her voice was barely a whisper.

"I think I'd better be going."

"No, don't." Becky reached across the table, pressing Dylan's wrist with the palm of her hand.

"I really have to go, Becky."

"I'm sorry." Then she gazed out across the school grounds, watching the young men and women make their way toward the old two-story brick building. "It's . . . I guess just being here brought back all those old memories of"—she took a deep breath—"of how things used to be . . . between us."

"That was a long time ago."

She nodded, then gave him a look of concern. "You're going to keep your job out at the site, aren't you?"

"I don't know, Becky."

"I promise it won't happen again." Her voice bordered on despair.

Dylan thought of how good it would feel to be out from under the debt that had been hanging over him and Susan since Erin's birth. "All right."

"Thanks, Dylan." She breathed a sigh of relief. "I don't know anybody else I can trust, and if I mess up this job . . . well, I'm afraid that would just about finish me."

"Don't worry about it." Dylan abbreviated his farewell to Becky and shook hands with Susslin as he left the store. Glancing back over his shoulder on the way to his car, he saw Becky staring out through the plate glass at the school. The sadness in her eyes seemed darker than the black shade beneath the old live oaks.

5

THE GNOME

Leaping down from the high wooden fence, Dylan sprinted through winter-dry leaves, his chest burning as he sucked the cold night air deep into his lungs. In the murky darkness of the backyards, he could see the shadowy figure, a dark-clothed wraith of a man, running ahead of him, clutching a small canvas bag in his left hand.

The chase had played itself out across what seemed to Dylan countless lawns and streets and alleyways, accompanied by the clanging of knocked-over garbage cans, a chorus of barking dogs, and shouts of neighbors. With every step he could feel the ever increasing pounding of his heart trying to rush enough oxygen through his bloodstream to maintain his speed against his elusive and apparently tireless quarry.

Dylan watched the little man ahead of him glance over his shoulder, his lips drawing back in a smile as though he knew he could easily outdistance his pursuer. As Dylan hurdled the low hedge, his legs aching and burning in protest, he saw the man suddenly go down, rolling and tumbling in the dark.

This is my last shot at him. If he gets up now I'm finished. Turning on a final burst of speed as the man began scrambling to his feet, Dylan leaped through the air, arms outstretched, hands grasping for a hold on an arm, leg, neck; it didn't matter as long as he didn't have to run anymore.

It was very close. The little man spun and twisted like a weasel. Dylan felt as though he were trying to hold on to a small, wiry tornado. Then he jammed his hand beneath the man's belt and got a firm hold.

"Stupid kids!" The little man spat the words out, his voice raspy and breathless.

Holding tightly to the belt, his legs now locked around the man's waist from behind, Dylan took several deep breaths, then said, "Is that you, Tut?"

"Who else?"

Dylan slipped his handcuffs from their case, snapped them on one wrist, and, twisting the other arm around, cuffed the man's hands behind his back. "I thought you'd gone back north."

"Too cold up there."

Dylan relaxed, leaning back on his elbows, until his labored breathing approached normal. He thought of the last time he had arrested Tutwell Ollie three years before for a series of petty thefts. Sent to a minimum security prison, he had gotten out in one year for exemplary behavior and had returned to his native Chicago. "What was that *stupid kids* remark about?"

"Look for yourself." Ollie nodded toward the route he had taken to his fall.

Dylan saw a tricycle tumbled on its side among the leaves. "God bless the little children."

"That's the trouble with this country. Kids got no respect for anything," Ollie grumbled. "My dad would have tanned my hide if I'd left my toys outside like that."

Dylan smiled at the little man's protests. "Do you see the irony of your words in this situation, Tut?"

"No, but I'd like to get my hands on that little brat for about two minutes. He'd never leave his toys outside again. You can bet on that."

"You know something, Tut?"

"Obviously not very much, if I let myself get caught by a Keystone Cop like you."

"That's a silly looking mask." After months of trying to catch the "Bicentennial Burglar," Dylan felt a giddiness welling up inside him now that it was over. "You remind me of a scruffy-looking, miniature Lone Ranger."

Ollie spoke directly into Dylan's laughter. "How'd you catch me, anyway?"

"I finally figured out your riddle." Dylan continued to laugh. "George Washington. You burglarized houses on streets that began with the letters of his name, in order. I'm surprised we didn't figure it out sooner."

"I'm surprised you figured it out at all."

"Did you know people were calling you the 'Bicentennial Burglar'?"

"Yeah." Ollie grinned behind his mask. "I heard about that. Kind of liked the sound of it, too."

Dylan felt recuperated enough to get to his feet. "You about ready to go home?"

"Home?"

"Jail," Dylan explained, pulling Ollie's mask off and sticking it in his pocket. "You obviously consider it your home; otherwise, why come back down here and let yourself get caught?"

Ollie gave him a sheepish grin. "You figured me out. Not bad for a cop."

Dylan thought the little man would have been a gnome in a world where gnomes existed. He took him beneath the armpits and helped him to his feet.

"You know the only thing I really dread about going back to jail?"

"No idea. What?" Dylan took him by the arm to lead him back to the car several blocks away.

Ollie balked.

"What's wrong now?"

67

Ollie nodded toward the canvas bag twenty feet away, half covered with leaves. "Don't forget my loot." He gave Dylan a conspiratorial wink. "Evidence, you know."

"Right." Dylan walked over and picked it up. Then as he crossed the yard toward the street, he asked, "Now, what's this thing you dread about jail, the food?"

"No, the forms. Having to answer all those questions so you cops can fill out all your forms."

"What's so bad about that?" Dylan marveled at the way the little man's mind worked, or maybe malfunctioned. "You don't have to fill them out."

Frowning, Ollie shuffled along next to Dylan. "I know that. You see, it's just that everybody always wants to correct me because my first name sounds like my last name and—"

"Your last name sounds like it should be your first name," Dylan finished for him.

"Exactly. You know how many different people I'm gonna have to explain that to?"

"What can I tell you, Ollie? It's a rough life."

On the way to the jail, Dylan listened to Ollie bring him up-to-date on his last three years. He was amazed at how many burglaries and thefts he had gotten away with in Chicago, if he was telling the truth, and tried to pin Ollie down on dates and places, but the little man only responded with his gnomelike smile.

Entering the jail, Dylan dropped the canvas bag on the duty officer's desk and uncuffed Ollie's hands. "Got a customer for you, Clovis."

Clovis Aubin, who had worked nights at the jail for as long as anyone could remember, including Emile, shambled out of the bathroom. His white crew-cut hair and smooth tanned face gave him a youthful appearance. "Well, well, if it ain't Ollie Tutwell. Sit down and let's get you registered."

Ollie complied after a little nudge from Dylan.

"Now, do you want a single or a double?" Aubin gave

Dylan a knowing smile. "And I guess you'll be wanting one of our new king-sized beds and a remote control television."

"Can we just cut the humor and get this over with?" Ollie grumbled.

"Suits me. Just trying to cheer you up a little." Aubin took a pad of forms from the desk, clicked his ballpoint, and asked, "Now, how do you spell your last name, Ollie?"

Ollie turned toward Dylan, a look of resignation on his thin face. "See what I mean?"

———

"Daddy, look at the tiger!" Erin, wearing a denim jumper and red cotton blouse, scampered away toward the huge open-air cage, its boulders and hills and bamboo-shaded concrete pool providing an inviting home for its single striped and fanged resident.

"Don't get too close, now, sweetheart." Susan slipped inside Dylan's arm as they followed along behind.

"How'd you like to have that much energy?" Dylan watched Erin on her tiptoes, struggling to see over the stone wall that kept visitors a safe distance from the cage proper. He stepped behind Erin, grabbed her beneath the arms, and plopped her down on the wall, his arms clasped protectively around her waist.

Erin watched the big cat pacing restlessly back and forth, its yellow eyes blazing in the shadows. A frown crinkled the flawless skin between her eyes. "What's he doing out here, Daddy?"

"This is where he lives."

"But we saw him out by the big stadium," she protested. "I thought that was where he lived."

Dylan smiled at Susan. "That was a different tiger at the stadium, sweetheart. His name is Mike, and he's the LSU mascot. You remember now?"

The frown went away. "Oh yes! Now I do." She pointed at

the cage. "What's *this* tiger's name?"

"Hmmm . . . let me see if I can remember." Dylan tapped the side of his head with one finger. "Is it . . . Rumplestiltskin?"

"No, Daddy. That's the little man who made gold from a pile of straw."

"Oh yeah, that's right. Well, I guess I don't know what the tiger's name is after all."

"What can I call it, then?"

"I've got a good name for it." Dylan cupped his hand and whispered in her ear.

Giggling, Erin glanced at her mother. "That's a good name. I like it."

Susan crossed her arms over her chest, staring down at her daughter. "And what's so funny, young lady?"

Erin giggled again, grinning at Dylan. "The tiger's got a funny name . . . Susan."

"Why, I think that's a very nice name for a tiger. Susan, Susan the Tiger. It's perfect."

Erin spotted a blue-and-white striped kiosk on the far side of the monkey island. A man with a white paper hat looked as though he was wilting before the onslaught of fifteen or twenty preschoolers screaming for peanuts, Cokes, popcorn, and cotton candy. "Can we go get some peanuts and Cokes?"

"Why don't we wait until the crowd thins a little," Susan suggested. "We'll look at the seals for a few minutes."

As Dylan and his family watched the seals' sleek torpedo quickness in the clear water, he felt his heart fill with gratitude for the peace and contentment that had come into his life. *Blessed beyond measure* were the words that leaped into his mind from some dim, half-remembered moment of his life. He offered up a silent prayer of thanksgiving to God who had so richly blessed him with Susan and Erin.

"This is where Mama and Daddy lived when we first got married, Erin." Susan pointed through the car window at the pale yellow cottage on Camellia Street near Baton Rouge's City Park. "Do you think it's pretty?"

Erin stared at the little house, then shrugged. "It's all right, I guess, but not as good as our place on the bayou." She gave her mother a puzzled look. "What do people do up here in Baton Rouge, Mama?"

"Oh," Susan began, caught off guard again by one of Erin's countless questions, "the same things we do, I suppose."

"But they don't have no—"

"Any, sugar," Susan interrupted, "they don't have any."

Erin blew her breath out between her lips. "Any, they don't have any boats to ride in and no place to fish . . . and no dock to jump into the water and swim, and no—"

"Look what they *do* have," Dylan interrupted, knowing Erin's litany of no's could go on as long as she had breath to produce them, "a playground."

"Where?" Erin's list forgotten, she glanced around wide-eyed for swings and sliding boards.

"Right down there." Dylan pointed toward the end of the next block. "Want to go try it out?"

"Can we?"

"Certainly." Dylan started the car, drove to the end of the block, parking at the curb beneath an ancient cedar, and let Erin out of the car.

Erin headed for the swings, her pale hair flying in the March breeze. At a more sedate pace, Susan followed her. Clambering onto the wooden seat of one of the chain swings, Erin waited for her mother to push her. Dylan could hear the sound of her voice, and even though he couldn't make out the words, he knew them by heart. "Push me higher, Mama."

As Dylan watched his child at play, he remembered other trips to the park when they lived in the little house on Camellia Street before Susan became pregnant. In the crisp, dry February air, he would sit on a bench beneath one of the old oaks and pretend he was watching his already born daughter at play. In his mind he had seen her as the image of her mother, dark-haired and green-eyed.

There she was, spilling headfirst down the slide onto the hard-packed ground at its bottom. Then she was up and running for the ladder in her yellow playsuit with Big Bird for a bib, and when she reached the top, the breeze fanned her hair out like a dark cloud around her face.

It seemed like only last week she was all stumbles and bruises. Today she moved among the other children with a surer step and a growing confidence in the climbs, swings, and turnings that are a child's prelude to grace. He wanted to keep her forever that age yet couldn't wait to see her move, a little awkwardly, down the stairs in a party dress and her first pair of high heels.

Dylan returned from his imaginings to the very real presence of Erin bounding onto his lap.

"Daddy, I'm hungry. Can we go to McDonald's?"

Gazing into her blue eyes, lighted with expectation, Dylan said, "You're so much better than my daydreams."

She frowned at him. "I don't understand."

"Sure we can go to McDonald's. It's my favorite place to eat in the whole world."

"I never expected to see you here." Dylan stared at Wes Kinchen walking toward him, still favoring his right knee that had been destroyed by a blindside block during his third year as middle linebacker at LSU. At six-five and proportioned like a sprinter, he was an imposing presence even in his unpressed tweed jacket and baggy khakis. When Wes lost his ability to play football, it left a hole in his life bigger than the ones he used to punch in offensive lines. The things he tried to fill it with only made more holes in different and more vital areas. "I heard you're with the state police now."

"Yep. I was in New Orleans on an undercover assignment when they had the last meeting." Wes pushed his shaggy red hair back from his face. "Anything happen worth mentioning?"

"They'll bring you up-to-date."

Wes tapped a Camel out of a pack he carried in his shirt pocket, flicked a kitchen match into flame with his thumbnail, and lit his cigarette. With smoke curling from his nostrils, he gawked at the Governor's Mansion. "This is some layout, ain't it?"

Dylan glanced at the white-columned mansion and shrugged. "It's all right, if you like these vulgar displays of money and privilege."

"Your place is bigger than this one, I guess?"

"Nah. It's about the size of one of their closets," Dylan muttered, "but done with taste. A kind of controlled Cajun elegance, I guess you'd say."

"I'd say that means you live in a tin-roofed shack on the bayou, then." Wes grinned. "That's what I'd say."

"Close."

Wes stuck a finger inside his collar, loosening it. "Neckties! Who conned men into thinking that a colored rag around your neck was fashion?"

"Same people who conned us into thinking that sucking poison into our lungs was fun."

Wes stared at the cigarette in his hand, dropped it on the ground, and stepped on it. "Why're we having this meeting here, anyway? I never heard of that happening before."

"I expect it's because he was elected on a get-tough-on-crime platform. Looks good in the news to have law enforcement folks meeting in his house. Just good politics." Dylan gazed at the men filing across the grounds into the mansion's back door. Representing law enforcement from several surrounding parishes, some wore suits and ties, some uniforms, but all possessed that flinty gaze of men who had seen too many sleepless nights and too many years of the things human beings are capable of doing after the sun goes down.

"Speaking of politics—"

"Tell me later, Wes. We'd better get inside."

"You need to know this," Wes insisted, "and I might forget about it later."

Dylan noticed the gaze in Wes's eyes harden slightly. "Somebody's got a score to settle with you."

Nodding toward the men passing them, Dylan said, "I expect you could say that about everybody here."

"This is a political score."

"You must be wrong. I left Baton Rouge seven years ago, and the three or four politicians in Evangeline are all pretty close friends of mine."

"I don't know the details. I got it second or thirdhand through the state police grapevine, but I did find out this much. It's an old score. Something that happened years back."

"Well, I don't think I can fit an old trouble onto my dance card. It's already full of new ones."

"You might at least think about taking it seriously," Wes offered.

"Okay, I'll think about it," Dylan relented. "What else can I do, anyway?"

"I don't know yet. I'll see what else I can find out." Wes gave Dylan a crooked smile. "You're not too busy to help out an old friend, are you?"

Dylan joined the stragglers heading into the mansion. "I don't like the sound of this already."

Wes fell in beside him. "You know I'd never get you into anything . . . unseemly, ol' buddy."

Remembering other "favors" he'd done for Wes when they worked together as parole officers, Dylan looked for a way out. "I don't have any jurisdiction here."

"Don't worry about that," Wes insisted. "My jurisdiction stops at Arkansas, Texas, Mississippi, and the Gulf of Mexico.

That covers you, too, when I ask for your assistance. See, no problem there. Now, as soon as this meeting's finished, we can have some fun."

"Whatever it is, I don't want to hear about it, Wes. I'm too old for your kind of fun." Dylan stepped through the back door and followed a long corridor, his boots making a thudding sound on the gleaming heart pine flooring. "I still remember that time you talked me into going after Odell Jackson with you."

"Funny you should mention him."

Dylan stopped and stared directly into Wes's slightly wild eyes. "Uh, uh. No way. Absolutely not!"

"Aw, c'mon, Dylan. It'll be like ol' times."

"Yeah, that's exactly why I'm not goin'."

"You'll love it."

"If you think I'd go chasing off with you after that nut case, you must be crazy."

———

"I *am* crazy," Dylan said, staring through the windshield of Wes's battered Chevrolet pickup. It bounced and rattled across the rutted gravel parking lot in front of the Green Dragon lounge, a squat block building situated in the shadow of I–10. "How'd I let you talk me into this?"

Wes parked behind a bright orange Dodge Charger, slapped the gearshift into reverse, and killed the engine. "I guess you should know Odell's bumped the ante."

"I don't think I want to know what that means."

"He's not a nickel-and-dime purse snatcher anymore." Wes pulled a stainless steel .357 from beneath his jacket, flicked the cylinder open, then slapped it shut.

"Oh yeah." Dylan felt a chill ripple down his spine. "What's he into now? Embezzling . . . tattooing minors?"

Wes laughed. "I'm glad to see you haven't lost your sense of humor."

Dylan stared at a man the size of a small Kodiac bear lumbering out of the Green Dragon. He squinted at them in the glare of sunlight, flashed his gold teeth, and got into a long yellow Cadillac, then showered gravel against the side of the truck as he spun out of the lot. "I think I'm gonna need more than a sense of humor on this one."

"Just follow my lead and you'll be all right."

Dylan noticed the wild gleam that had come into Wes's eyes. "I remember asking you a question in this same parking lot seven years ago, Wes. You never gave me an answer."

"What was the question?"

"Are you familiar with the term *Death Wish*?"

"That's a good one, Dylan," Wes said in a flat tone. "You got a piece with you?"

"Yep." Dylan pulled his trouser leg up, slipped a five-shot Smith & Wesson revolver from an ankle holster, and checked the cylinder, then shoved the pistol inside his waistband. "I'm all out of hand grenades, though."

"That's all right," Wes grinned. "I've got plenty."

His heart pounding, the palms of his hands burning slightly as they had done years before in Vietnam, Dylan walked next to Wes toward the paintless front door.

James Brown shrieked from the jukebox as they entered the dark, roaring bedlam of the Green Dragon. Blue-white smoke hung in the stale air like a thick fog. The jukebox and lights from several whiskey and beer signs provided the only illumination. Couples crowded the tiny dance floor or sat together in the booths along both side walls. A half-dozen men wearing dark clothes and bright jewelry sat on barstools at the far end.

"Nice place, huh," Wes muttered.

"Yeah, I expect the governor'll be along any minute now."

Wes sauntered across the room and sat down on a padded stool at the end of the bar. Dylan followed and stood next to him, facing the door.

Giving the men lined up along the bar a slightly insane

smile, Wes said, "Well, boys, when the rest of the troops get here, we're gonna shake everybody down for drugs and weapons. 'Course, since y'all are CEOs and ministers of the Gospel, there shouldn't be any problem here."

Muttering obscenities among themselves, all the men gave Wes and Dylan oblique glances of manufactured contempt, then got up and shuffled off toward the front door.

Dylan turned to the barmaid. She wore thigh-high boots, a black leather skirt, and a remote expression. Expecting to get a barrage of nonanswers, he said, "We're looking for Odell Jackson. Know where he is?"

She held a shot glass up to the light of a Pabst Blue Ribbon sign, seemed satisfied, then merely nodded toward the last booth along the far wall.

Wes had almost covered the distance across the room before Dylan finished his "thank you" to the barmaid.

"This is too good to be true," Wes said, staring at the shadowy booth.

Dylan walked over and stood next to him. An almost empty bottle of Crown Royal, its purple velvet bag discarded, sat on the table along with two smudged glasses. Odell, passed out on the bench, his head propped crookedly against the wall, smelled as though he had bathed in a vat of whiskey.

Breathing a sigh of relief, Dylan asked, "You never did tell me why you're after Odell."

Wes grabbed Odell's purple jacket and pulled him upright in the seat. Then he patted him down, finding a .380 automatic and a ten-inch switchblade. Handing them to Dylan, he cuffed Odell's hands behind his back and let him slide back against the wall.

Dylan was about to ask his question again when he heard an almost inhuman shrieking from behind him. Glancing over his shoulder, he saw a woman in a red dress and spiked heels, a thin-bladed knife in her raised fist, running clumsily at Wes, who was still facing Odell.

"Wes, behind you!" Dylan dropped the .380 and switch-blade, turning to intercept the woman. Before he could stop her he saw a blur of motion as Wes pulled his pistol, turned in one smooth motion, and slapped the heavy barrel against the side of the woman's head. She dropped like a rock.

Wes jammed the pistol back in its holster, then stared down at the unconscious woman at his feet. "Bargain day at the Green Dragon." He grinned at Dylan. "Two for the price of one."

PART TWO

ERIN

6

THE DEAL GOES DOWN

Dylan sat on the weathered cypress decking, leaning back against a piling that supported the dock. Susan, idly running her fingers through his dark hair, sat next to him in a nylon-webbed aluminum chair.

A thin band of clouds above the tree line on the opposite side of the bayou glowed with colors of peach and slate blue. Redear bream, their round mouths making soft plopping sounds, fed in the shallows beneath the pale green cascade of a weeping willow.

"How'd the meeting go?" Susan gazed at the dented surface of the bayou where the fish were feeding.

"Not much different than last time. The press didn't show up at that one, though. Somebody forgot to notify them, so this was basically a repeat performance so the governor could get his photos for the newspaper and television; show everybody he's carrying out his campaign promises."

"You ready for coffee?"

"I'll get it." Dylan got up, crossed the narrow, handrailed bridge from the dock over to their gallery, and went inside the cabin. Pouring the freshly dripped coffee, he added sugar to his and cream to Susan's. Then, taking his shoes off, he quietly walked down the hall and looked into Erin's room. She sat at her desk, her pale hair gleaming in the light through the window, engrossed in her latest book, *Peter Cottontail*. Dylan watched her for a full minute, then carried the coffee back out to the dock.

Taking her cup, Susan asked, "She still reading?"

Dylan nodded and sipped the rich, dark brew. "She read a whole page out loud to me last night."

"Maybe she'll be a teacher like her mother was," Susan suggested, "that is, until her daddy made a full-time Cajun wife out of me."

But Dylan was already lost in thought.

"Am I having this conversation by myself?"

"Oh, sorry." He took a swallow of coffee. "I was just thinking about Wes."

"What about him?"

Dylan took his place next to the piling. "Vicki left him four years ago. Moved back to Ruston where her parents live. He said he hardly ever sees Chet."

"He must be nine or ten by now."

"Twelve," Dylan said, remembering the desolation that his life became when Susan had left him years before.

"That's hard on a boy to lose his father like that. It's almost like he died."

"I don't think he has many friends. He's been doing undercover work for the state police for a long time now . . . maybe too long. They tend to overuse the men who don't have families or, like Wes, who aren't with them." Dylan reluctantly told her about the incident at the Green Dragon.

"Don't you have enough of your own work without putting yourself through that?"

Dylan thoughtfully rubbed his temple with his fingertips. "I'm not sure he could get anybody else to go with him. Not on such short notice, anyway."

"Does he. . . ?"

"No, he's not on the pills anymore," Dylan answered, shaking his head slowly. "Said he quit a few months ago."

"Maybe he could get his marriage back together then," Susan said hopefully.

"Maybe. I even suggested it to him, but he just pushed the whole thing aside. Didn't want to talk about it." Dylan thought about Wes's warning, but felt there probably wasn't anything to it and decided it would only worry Susan needlessly if he told her. "He's leading a lonely life, Susan."

"Why don't you ask him to supper. I doubt he gets many home-cooked meals."

"I'll do that." Dylan yawned, stretching his arms above his head. "Right now, I'm going to catch a nap."

"You want to eat first?"

Dylan shook his head. "I've got to go out later. Make a quick run through some of the main channels for drug traffic. Then I'm going to check on the movie site." He smiled into Susan's concerned look. "Don't worry. It won't take long."

"The last time you went out there . . . she came out there, too, didn't she?"

"I told you about that." Dylan stood up, taking Susan's hand and lifting her out of the chair.

Susan slipped her arm around his waist. "Something bothers me about this whole thing."

"Susan, that was a long time ago," Dylan assured her. "We were just kids."

"It's not that." Susan gazed at the rose-colored afterglow lighting the western sky. "Something bothers me about this whole business." She gathered up their cups and saucers, placing them on the tray. "It's . . . I don't know what it is exactly, but something's not right."

"Forget about it." Dylan kissed her on the forehead. "There's enough real trouble in this ol' world without worrying about something that doesn't exist."

Susan gazed into his eyes, then gave him a halfhearted smile, nodding her head. "Maybe you're right."

"C'mon then. I want to hear Erin read another page before I sack out." He took the tray from her and headed across the walkway toward the cabin.

Susan glanced back at the light, fading quickly now above the Basin, then hurried after her husband.

———

Dylan sat on the cushioned seat of the speedboat, which was tied to a cypress knee in the mouth of a sluggish bayou that joined one of the countless canals dredged by the oil companies. Hunters, fishermen, and smugglers preferred them to the natural channels because they were usually clear of obstructions and because they ran straight instead of meandering through the Basin. Far above him a fingernail sliver of moon hung in a cloudless sky.

Looks like I'm out of luck tonight. Another ten minutes, then a quick run by the village site and home to bed. Dylan poured an inch of black coffee into the thermos's plastic cup. Sipping it, he listened to the faint, distant whine of a diesel truck on one of the back roads they would never travel during daylight hours.

Dylan zipped his jacket against the March chill and rested his head on the seat. Alone in the vast Louisiana wetlands, it seemed as though his memories always took him to a time in another wet country on the far side of the world.

Corporal Vince Cannelli, a stocky, curly-haired baker from Queens and Dylan's best friend since boot camp, pulled the jeep to a stop next to the river. The command post across the road was housed in a large block building fortified with sandbags. Several malnourished dogs lazed in the afternoon sunshine. ARVN soldiers in their tiger-striped fatigues sat in groups of four or five around their foxholes, talking and playing cards.

Cannelli fished a pack of Camels from his pocket, tapped one out, and stuck it in the corner of his mouth. "These guys got it too easy. Somebody ought to drag them out in the boonies for a month or two so they can find out what this war's all about."

Opening his canteen, Dylan turned it up and let the tepid water slosh down his throat. "I'd let 'em stay right where they are for one good-sized block of ice."

"I'm going over there and pick up a couple packs of cigarettes. You want something?"

Dylan glanced across the road. Next to the command post, women in pajama-like clothes and straw hats sold fish, rice, tea, bananas, and other items out of open-air, thatched-roof stalls. Even at this distance he could see black clouds of flies hovering around their tables. "No thanks. Just don't take all day. I want to get out of this place."

"What's your hurry?"

"I don't know. It spooks me, that's all."

Cannelli, the unlit cigarette dangling from his lips, plodded across the dusty road. He called back over his shoulder, "Sure I can't bring you back a bowl of stewed fish heads?"

Dylan grinned and shook his head. Slouching down against the seat, he closed his eyes, imagining himself in the air-conditioned Walgreen Drugstore on Canal Street drinking a cold, thick chocolate malt.

A few seconds later, Dylan opened his eyes. At first he thought he had drifted off to sleep or was seeing an apparition. Then the noise and the heat told him it was all real. She looked as cool and remote as an Alpine wildflower in her flowing white tunic. Her eyes were big and dark in her bright, childlike face. She walked directly over to Cannelli and stood behind him until he turned around. His white teeth gleamed in his swarthy face as he engaged her in animated conversation.

Five minutes later Dylan watched them walk together toward a small hooch located beyond the marketplace near the jungle. He felt a slight chill at the back of his neck in spite of the blistering sun. Slinging the M–16 over his shoulder, he walked across the road and bought a cup of hot tea, staring at the hooch while he drank it. Then he followed the path Cannelli had taken, stopping at the door next to a smoldering charcoal pit.

"Cannelli! You 'bout ready to get out of here?" He waited a few seconds but heard nothing. "Cannelli . . ."

85

Dylan unslung the M–16, flicking the safety to automatic fire. Using the barrel of the rifle, he pushed aside the curtain door. No movement . . . no sound from the shadowy interior. He cautiously followed the muzzle of his rifle into the hooch.

Cannelli lay motionless on his back on a straw mat on the dirt floor. Dylan knelt next to him, staring at the thin knife buried to its delicate ivory hilt in his chest, then he touched the pool of blood that had crimsoned the thin straw mat.

Leaping to his feet in a sudden rage, Dylan burst through the back door, searched the path to the edge of the jungle, firing a full clip out into its brooding darkness. He ran back to the marketplace, screaming incoherently at everyone he saw. Swinging his rifle by the barrel, he destroyed two of the stalls before his rage was spent.

Slowly, his head cleared. Ten months "in country" told him that the girl had vanished and that he would never see her again. He walked back to the hooch, went inside, and sat down next to his friend. Twenty minutes later the MPs came and took them away.

It was the last time Dylan would call back the memory of his friend's death. From that moment on he only remembered Cannelli as alive, engaged in some outrageous prank in the rear areas or rock-solid next to him in battle.

Screwing the top back on the thermos, Dylan loosed the tether from the cypress knee, started the engine, and flicked on the running lights. As he eased the throttle forward, a sudden *thunk* startled him, followed instantly by the sharp crack of a rifle. Cutting the engine and lights, he saw a round hole in the plastic windshield six inches to the left of his head.

Dylan grabbed the M–16, stepped over the gunwale onto a huge cypress root, and settled himself into shooting position. Then he reached over and flicked the lights on, shouldered his rifle, and waited for the sniper's muzzle flash as his target. But no second shot was fired . . . only silence followed. Cold and tired, and convinced the shooter was gone, he finally climbed back into the boat, turned the lights off, and started the engine, running out into the channel by starlight.

Dylan shoved the throttle forward, able to see the outline of the bayou now by the glow of the village lights. He pulled into the dock, got out, and walked around the movie site. Everything looked normal: the stacks of lumber and other building materials undisturbed; the doors securely bolted and padlocked on the buildings that housed tools and electrical equipment.

Hopping up on a stack of two-by-fours, Dylan let his legs dangle over the edge and his eyes wander about the emerging village. Most of the cabins had been roofed with composite shingles made to look like rough, hand-hewn cypress. The little church stood at the far end next to the forest and across from a mock bayou that had been dug with a backhoe. Some of the fake weathering had been applied to the siding and shingles, giving the houses the appearance of years of aging in the blazing heat and incessant rain of South Louisiana.

Dylan could almost see a true village of more than two hundred years before. The women boiling clothes in huge black pots; men coming home from the woods and waters of the Basin with fish and game for supper; children playing beneath the old trees in their homespun clothes. Then the whine of an approaching outboard brought him back to his own century.

Unslinging his M–16 from his shoulder, Dylan leaped down and stepped behind the stack of lumber. In his mind he could see the round hole punched in the windshield of his boat. Then he relaxed as the boat pulled close, letting his breath out in a rush. *What's she doing out here this time of night?*

"Dylan . . . Dylan, where are you?" Becky, wearing a heavy parka and carrying an insulated pouch, stepped onto the dock and peered out into the dusty light.

Dylan stepped out from behind the lumber stack and walked over the rutted ground littered with scraps of boards and other castoffs of the building trade. "Becky, it's two o'clock in the morning."

"Do you go *bong, bong,* too, or do you just announce the time hourly?"

"Why are you out here? Don't you know it's dangerous to go traipsin' around in the swamps at night?"

"No questions, please," Becky insisted, placing two cups on the dock and pouring coffee from a thermos bottle. "My mind isn't functioning properly yet."

Dylan sat down on the dock six feet from the edge of the bayou, his feet on the spongy ground. "This isn't a good idea, Becky . . . for more reasons than one."

Becky stopped the thermos halfway to the second cup, holding it at an angle, steam rising from its mouth. "You mean you don't want me here . . . with you?" Her lips went pale and an old sorrow seemed to bleed darkness into her eyes.

Embarrassed now, Dylan tried to make amends. "I'm sorry. I guess that sounded pretty rough." He glanced at the hole in the windshield of the boat on the opposite side of the dock. "It's just that . . . maybe we shouldn't be out here, just the two of us together like this."

Resuming her pouring, Becky filled the second cup. "You mean your wife wouldn't like it if she found out?"

"No, that's not it at all. She already knows."

"She does? How?"

"I told her," Dylan replied, wondering why Becky seemed to feel there was something to hide. "How else?"

"You mean you told her about . . . about us?"

"Becky, there's nothing to tell, except that we've spent some time together because of the work."

Becky appeared to be surprised by Dylan's words. "I guess you're right at that." She gave Dylan a sad smile. "I guess because I've changed so much since school, I sometimes think everybody else has, too."

"We all change."

"Not you. Not deep down where it really counts." She couldn't hold his gaze now and let her eyes wander toward the village. "You haven't changed at all."

"I don't really know what you're talking about."

"When we were going steady, you were always true to me, weren't you?"

"I guess so."

"You *know* so," Becky corrected him quickly. Her eyes seemed to stare back through the years. "And you remember how a bunch of us would take the ferry across to Canal Street on Saturday mornings?"

"Sure."

"And some of the boys," Becky continued, "would steal candy or chewing gum from Woolworth's."

"Yeah, I remember."

"You never would."

"So."

"That's what I'm talking about. You haven't changed. You're still like that."

"You're right. I always pay for Erin's candy when I take her to the five-and-dime."

Becky ignored his remark. Her gaze had lost the faraway look of the past. "Here, drink your coffee."

"I better get goin'."

Reaching into the pouch, she took out two muffins and placed them on napkins. "I baked them myself. They're blueberry, and they're still warm."

"Becky, I—"

"Oh, hush! You're not going to do anything wrong, so just quit talking and eat."

Dylan smiled. "I guess you're right." He took a bite, chewed hungrily, and drank some of the coffee. "Aren't you going to have one?"

Becky stared off into the night. "No. I don't seem to have much of an appetite anymore."

———

Dylan rode a warm current through a soft, enfolding darkness. He felt himself beyond the touch of time, at one with the silent, whirling planets and the windless stars. Lights glimmered and twinkled at the remote edges of this new world, then suddenly rushed at him, exploding inside his head with a blinding, hot white pain. Nausea swept over him in waves.

Groaning, Dylan struggled to open his eyes. They refused, as though someone had glued them shut. His arms and legs felt as weak as an invalid's. Suddenly the nausea wracked his body. Retching, he forced himself over on his side to keep from choking. Then he dropped down, down into a bottomless ocean of darkness and cold and unthinkable horror.

"Susan . . ." Ages had whirled past in a dazzle of light; civilizations had come and gone in Dylan's new world. "Susan . . ." He felt for her, his hand sliding along the cool, white sheet, then he opened his eyes slowly. Pain shut them. He tried to move, but his numbed brain sent only sluggish, unreadable signals.

A crashing sound; wood splintering and the thudding of something heavy. Rough hands grabbed him, arms twisted behind his back. Disembodied voices sounded as though from a great distance. Gripped beneath his arms, he felt himself dragged along a smooth floor, then down stairs. Forcing his eyes open, he glimpsed white columns, galleries, and the distant gleam of the river. *The Pentagon.*

———

Sitting up on the lumpy mattress, Dylan stared at its striped ticking, stained and soiled by countless men who had lain there before him. Then he rested his head in both hands, waiting for the dizziness to subside. Placing the flat of his hands on the mattress, he opened his eyes again.

Pale light slanted through the narrow rectangle in the solid iron door. A foul liquid was pooled in small hollows of the rough concrete next to an open hole. The smell of unwashed bodies, urine, and human fear permeated the stale, dank air of the cell.

Dylan heard the distinctive *buzz-clank* of electric doors being opened and closed. *Four doors. . . . I must be at the bottom of the food chain back here.*

Keys clacked in the lock of his cell. The heavy door swung slowly open. "You got ten minutes, Sheriff," someone said in a whiskey rasp.

Emile stepped into the cell, blinking his eyes against the gloom. The door thudded shut behind him. He glanced around the cell, then stared down at Dylan. "You should have asked for the corporate rate."

Forcing a smile, Dylan muttered, "I'm afraid they didn't give me much choice."

Emile sat down on the battered iron bunk. "Somebody's certainly done a number on you this time, Dylan . . . made you look like a real naughty boy."

"You're gonna have to bring me up-to-date," Dylan admitted, rubbing the back of his neck. "I remember being out in the swamp, then two or three men carried me"—an image of the limestone walls of the Capitol building towering against a blue afternoon sky flashed in Dylan's muddled memory—"out of the Pentagon. . . . I think that's where it was."

"You're right. You were in your old schoolmate's bed, to be precise."

"I was in her bed? Where was she?"

"Nobody's been able to locate her yet."

"How'd I get there?"

"I was hoping you could tell me."

Dylan shook his head slowly, thinking now only of Susan. *How could she ever accept this? She'd never believe such a wild story.* "Tell me everything you know about this, Emile. I was supposed to be home by 3 A.M. I remember telling Susan that when I left for the Basin."

"When you didn't show, she called us around five this morning. We started a search and found the boat about a mile down the bayou from your house."

"Why'd they jail me?"

"You really don't remember anything, do you? The arresting officer told me he gave you Miranda rights and offered to let you make a phone call."

"I must have been on Pluto about that time. I get glimpses of bits and pieces, but none of it makes any sense."

"Drugs," Emile said flatly, making a face at the hole-in-the-floor bathroom. "That's what they charged you with. But it's just possession and not intent to distribute . . . yet. Said they found a dozen ampules of morphine in your jacket along with a small bag of pills." He took a deep breath. "And we found a bundle of grass stashed away in the boat, Dylan."

A sudden sinking feeling hit Dylan in the pit of his stomach. "They did a number on me, all right. You don't believe I had anything to do with this do you, Emile?"

"I won't let myself get offended at that question because I know you're not making any sense right now, but don't say stupid things like that from now on." Emile stood up and paced the short span of floor. "They must have been waiting for you in the shed at your house. Somehow they knocked you out." He stopped and glanced down at Dylan. "You don't have a lump on your head anywhere, do you?"

"It only hurts from the inside," Dylan muttered, feeling his head with his fingertips. "I guess they could have hit me with something like one of those leather saps filled with sand, something that wouldn't leave a knot." He held his head in both hands. "Something gave me this headache."

"Ether maybe," Emile suggested. "Anyway, the doctor found chloral hydrate and morphine in your system. The morphine must have been used after you were unconscious." His brow furrowed in thought. "And the chloral hydrate alone could have put you under, if there was enough of it."

"I remember checking at the village"—Dylan propped his elbows on his knees and clasped his hands together—"and I think Becky came and gave me something to eat. Everything's really foggy now."

"Maybe she saw something . . . or somebody," Emile said, sitting back down on the bunk. "In any case, it's a place to start. She's the last person you remember seeing . . . *and* you were found in her apartment."

"She's the obvious one to frame me with. Whoever did this took a while to set it up right." Dylan shook his head slowly back and forth. "How can I ever explain this to Susan? She tried to warn me about Becky."

"You don't have to explain anything. All you have to do is tell her what happened."

"I don't know, Emile." Dylan remembered years back when he had lost Susan's trust, having treated their marriage with a trifling disuse. "I know husbands and wives have to trust each other, but this is really pushing the limit."

Emile shook his head sadly. "It's just one of those situations the two of you will have to get through together. She wanted to come with me, but I wouldn't let her." He glanced at Dylan's hollow-eyed, unshaven face and stained, wrinkled clothes. "I'm sure glad I didn't let her."

"Yeah, seeing me like this wouldn't do either of us any good." Dylan felt a sense of relief wash over him and a deep sense of gratitude toward his friend. "What about—"

"We'll talk this all out later," Emile interrupted him. "Let's get out of here now. They ought to have you about checked out up at the front desk."

"How much was bail?"

"They let me sign you out. Even a low-level politician like me has some clout in this state." Emile's face darkened. "One other thing, then we'll get you home and decide what to do."

Dylan felt a sudden chill like a sliver of ice in his chest. "Erin's all right. . . ."

"Sure." Emile clapped him on the shoulder. "Settle down, she's fine."

"What is it then?"

"The charges against you, including the circumstances of your arrest, are going in the newspaper. They're not going to splash it all over the front page, though. I found out that much."

"Oh no," Dylan whispered, shaking his aching head. Still, knowing that Susan and Erin were unharmed seemed to be enough for the moment. "I can see it now," he added, no trace of humor in the tone of his voice, 'Local Boy Makes Good.'

"You're gonna be all right," Emile said, standing up and brushing his clothes off. "Let's go home."

7

MATTIE

Emile pulled the white Chevy Blazer off the blacktop, parking on a grassy spot between the shed and the cabin. He turned off the engine and looked at the sunlight winking on the bayou. "You go on in and see Susan. I'll be along in a little while."

"Sure you don't want to come on in with me?" Knowing what he had to face Susan with, Dylan felt he could use a friend standing next to him.

"No. You and Susan need a little time to yourselves right now. I'll make a call or two, then walk on down to the dock and enjoy the sunshine."

Dylan leaned over, glancing into the rearview mirror. Emile had stopped at the office so he could shower, shave, and put on the extra uniform he kept there, but he thought he still had the appearance of an invalid who was just beginning to show signs of improvement. "I'll be down in a little while then."

Emile placed a hand on Dylan's shoulder as he was getting out of the Blazer. "It's gonna be all right, son."

Dylan nodded, stepped out into the cool March air, and walked down the slope toward home. Looking back, he saw that Emile was already talking to someone on the radio.

Just as he reached the path running from the shed to the cabin, Susan burst through the kitchen door, ran across the gallery and down the steps, rushing into Dylan's arms. "Oh, Dylan, I'm so glad you're home!"

Dylan felt a great relief flooding through him. He knew then that everything truly was all right between him and Susan, and he realized that he could endure losing his job or even his freedom as long as he had Susan and Erin. "I'm kinda glad about it myself."

"Thank God, you're all right!"

Dylan held her close, feeling her warm breath against his neck, the touch of her lips on his, breathing in the fragrance of her hair. He found that the doubts that had tormented him since he came to consciousness in that dank and lonely cell could not exist in the circle of their arms.

"Well, I finally got Erin down for a nap," Susan said, placing the coffee service on a wooden table. "She was so exhausted, she'll probably sleep all night."

Emile picked up one of the cups and sipped the rich, dark coffee. "I found out from one of the secretaries in the Tourism Department that Becky flew back to California on business. That may be true. According to the lady I talked to, she makes about one trip a week out there. In any case, the police in Baton Rouge are going to want her back here for questioning."

"I'd like to talk to her myself," Dylan said, remembering her last visit to him out in the swamp.

"You think she's involved in setting you up, Dylan?" Emile slipped a notepad from inside his jacket and flipped through a few pages. "We've already run a check on her, and she's got a clean record in California—a couple of speeding tickets, but that's all. Same in Louisiana."

Susan sat down in a cypress rocker next to Dylan. "I can't believe she'd get involved in something like this from what

you've told me about her." She glanced at Dylan's weary looking face. "After all, the two of you have been friends for years."

Dylan nodded. "Like I told you, that was a long time ago.
I'll feel better after I talk to her."

"The Baton Rouge PD are checking the whole area
around the Pentagon and the Capitol. Maybe they'll come up
with somebody who saw something." Emile put his notepad
away. "A night watchman . . . anybody."

"You think they believe I was set up?"

"Any cop with one eye and half a brain can see that's exactly what it was." Emile gave him a half-smile. "Some of them
are on your side. If anybody saw what happened, they'll find
it out." He drained his coffee cup and set it on the deck next
to his chair. " 'Course, some of them aren't especially fond of
you either."

"You can't please everybody, I guess," Dylan said, his voice
slightly hoarse.

"I think we ought to talk with Susan now," Emile said.
"Then I have to leave. I've got a few calls out that I ought to
be getting answers for pretty soon."

"Talk to me about what?" Susan's voice held a slight edge
of alarm.

"Someone took a shot at Dylan."

"When?"

"Last night." Dylan took her hand, giving it a reassuring
squeeze. "It might have been a wild shot from somebody
poaching deer."

"Maybe," Emile said, "but I think we ought to take the
necessary precautions, anyway. Besides, why would whoever it
is try to take you off the board just a couple of hours before
they set you up on a drug charge?"

"Beats me," Dylan said. "None of this makes any sense to
me now, though."

"Emile, what does this 'necessary precautions' mean?"
Susan asked.

"Maybe I'd better answer that." Dylan took both of Susan's hands, staring into her eyes. "I want you to take Erin to New Orleans and stay with your mother for as long as it takes to get this mess cleared up."

"I'm not going to leave my home," Susan protested. "Besides, you need me here with you."

"I need you where I know you'll be safe. I have to get to work on my own and find out who's responsible for this so we can get our lives back to normal."

Susan's face took on a puzzled frown. "What do you mean by 'on your own'?"

"I had to suspend him, Susan." Emile spoke in a low, level tone, his expression stoic. "Any officer with criminal charges filed against him is suspended until the case is cleared. I didn't have any choice in the matter." He glanced at Dylan. "Of course, there's no law against an ordinary citizen asking questions, digging into things on his own. And . . . unofficially, of course . . . he might even get help from friends in law enforcement."

Dylan knew well the implications of Emile's statement. He reached into his jacket, took out his detective's shield, and handed it to Emile. Then he slipped his Colt out of its holster, holding it toward him butt first.

Emile waved him away. "You keep the weapon. The department has nothing to do with a pistol I gave you. You do remember that, don't you, and Jack Ryder blasting your old one with that AK–47."

Dylan saw again the snowy, windswept mountaintop in Arizona. "Hard to forget that."

"I gotta go." Emile stood up, kissed Susan on the cheek, then rested his hand on Dylan's shoulder. "We're going to get your life back together. I'll see that a patrol unit gets by here pretty often to check on things." He turned again to Susan. "Try not to fret too much about all of this."

"We're blessed to have a friend like Emile," Susan said,

watching him walk up the slope toward his Blazer.

Even dreading the things he knew he must do, Dylan felt that his own will was strengthened by the knowledge that Emile was standing with him. "Let's go get you and Erin packed. The sooner you get away from here, the better."

"You don't really think anyone would come to our home? They must know you'll be ready for them now."

"Probably not," Dylan answered to ease Susan's worries, although his words sounded hollow in his own ears, "but there are never any pat answers for situations like this. You haven't seen your mother in a while, anyway, so just pretend it's a vacation and try to enjoy yourself."

"I do feel better knowing Emile's going to keep an eye on you," Susan admitted.

"I've been needing a little time off myself," Dylan said, trying to sound as though he had nothing to do but lie around and soak up the spring sunshine. Dylan watched Emile pull onto the blacktop and drive away. Susan stood next to him, her arm around his waist, but he felt at that moment . . . forsaken. The words seemed to rise unbidden from his heart. *God, you know I've tried my best to live for You since that time in the hospital when we didn't know if Erin was going to live or die. Why have You let this terrible time come to my family?*

———————

"Daddy, I want you to come, too." Erin held Dylan's hand as she walked down the steps from the gallery. "We can go ride on the ferryboat and everything."

Carrying a suitcase, Dylan lifted her in his free arm. "I have to stay and work, sweetheart. You and Mommy are going to have a big time, though, and maybe I'll be able to come down real soon."

Erin's blue eyes clouded with a passing sadness, then she said, "Put me down."

"Are you too big for Daddy to carry you anymore?" Dylan

placed her on the path leading to the shed.

"Watch how fast I can run in my new shoes."

Dylan watched the little blue-and-yellow tennis shoes flashing in the morning sunlight as she hurried along the path and through the door into the shed. Catching up with her, he said, "My goodness, you *are* fast! Why, I'll bet you could catch a bunny rabbit if he didn't run into a briar patch."

"Bet I could, too."

Walking around to the back of the Ford station wagon, where Susan was loading a few of Erin's books and toys, Dylan placed the suitcase into the storage area. Then he looked at Susan in her pleated skirt and jade green blouse. "You look especially elegant today."

Straightening up from her task, Susan placed her hands on Dylan's shoulders. "Why, thank you, sir." She kissed him on the lips. "We women in our thirties are awfully fond of compliments."

Dylan gazed at the fragile curves and turnings of his wife's face, her lips holding a delicate rose color of their own, and he thought her as radiant as a bride. "Be careful down there. You know how crazy those people drive."

She nodded. "I'm going to miss you."

Erin scrambled in between them. "Me, too, Daddy!"

Smiling down at his daughter, Dylan picked her up, carried her around to the passenger side door, and placed her on the seat. "You mind Mommy now and be a sweet girl."

Erin stood up on the seat and gave him a hug. "I will, Daddy. You be good, too."

Dylan kissed her on the cheek, walked around the car, and opened the door for Susan. Taking her in his arms, he held her close, feeling the comfort that always came with her touch. Then he kissed her and let her slide behind the wheel.

Susan started the engine, then looked up at him. "Be sure and thank Emile for letting us use his car."

"I will."

"There's plenty cooked," Susan said, repeating her instructions of ten minutes before. "All you have to do is warm it."

Dylan nodded. He had run out of words.

"One more kiss." Susan leaned over and kissed him, then backed out of the shed.

Following them out to the blacktop, Dylan stood in the white shells at the side of the road and waved a final good-bye, then watched them until they disappeared around a curve in the shade of overhanging trees.

As he stood in a world flooded by pale gold sunshine, Dylan felt a sudden, almost overwhelming, sense of desolation. It left him empty and hollow, filled with a gnawing despair. *How can I support my family? Who's going to take care of them if . . . if I'm locked up in prison?* With a final glance down the road, he walked back to the cabin, sat down on the porch swing, and stared out at the sunlight glittering on the bayou.

Clouds climbed the southern horizon, blotting out the sun as Dylan sat alone trying to think his way out of his troubles. Time had lost meaning for him. He seemed cut off from the world by a wall of darkness. Relentlessly bitter thoughts forced themselves toward the forefront of his consciousness. *Why would Susan stay with a man who can't even support his family? Especially a man with a criminal record.* He remembered in exquisite detail that terrible morning seven years earlier when, under circumstances of his own making, she had left him.

Susan wore a black pleated skirt and a white silk blouse. Black pumps and sheer stockings accentuated her long legs and slim ankles. It brought the same old sweet ache to his chest just seeing her. Dylan felt without any words forming themselves in his mind that all man would ever know of woman was there at that moment, evanescent and eternal.

But in the causal trifling ease with which he had treated their marriage, he had finally crossed a line. He wanted to beg her not to leave, to shout at her not to do this to them, but he could not.

Gathering up her coat and overnight bag, Susan walked quickly to the door of his apartment. Then she turned, a whisper of a smile crossing her face. "You know what I remember about you that night we met? The way your eyes smiled . . . even when you didn't. I remember how blue and happy they looked."

Her face lost its momentary control over the fixed expression. "And there was a gentleness in them then. Now there's something . . . different."

With Susan's words still weighing on him like a stone, Dylan watched her vanish . . . no glancing back, no slight hesitation as she crossed the threshold.

Dylan came back from his waking nightmare to the sound of raindrops pinging on the air conditioner cover behind him. A chill wind blew across the water. Rain came down harder, churning the bayou's surface a frothy white.

Staring out at the misty gray curtain of rain, Dylan marveled that the weather could turn around so quickly. Then he got up and went into the kitchen. *Three o'clock! I've been sitting out there for seven hours. You've made a great start at taking care of your problems, Dylan.* Feeling an urgency to do something . . . anything, he found his mind so muddled he couldn't make a beginning, not just yet, anyway.

Walking back to their bedroom, Dylan took a gray *LSU Tennis* sweatshirt from his chest of drawers and slipped it on. Then he went back to the gallery and stepped out into the cold spray blowing in beneath the tin roof. Sitting down in the swing, he watched the rain blowing against the dark sheen of the trees and the reeds swaying in the wind at the water's edge.

––––––––––

Dylan hardly noticed the rolling hills and pine trees of Feliciana pass by through the Volkswagen's windshield as he listened to Ronnie Milsap sing "A Legend in My Time." The mellow voice sounded tinny through the little dashboard speaker.

Turning into the old home place, Dylan listened to the slow

crunching of gravel beneath his tires. He stopped the car, shoved the gearshift into neutral, and got out. To his left a well-worn path led back to a tin-roofed shack that faced the main road. In front of him the gravel drive led due west toward the river. Huge trees formed a canopy eighty feet above him. Sunlight striking the new spring leaves cascaded downward in pale gold streams.

Dylan gazed down the road that led to the cottage hidden in the deep woods and on past it toward the river. He remembered the coolness of that quiet, shady tunnel on hot summer days when he would come up from New Orleans to visit his grandparents. Climbing back into the Volkswagen, he drove through the open gate and into his past.

Turning off the driveway, Dylan crossed a culvert over a creek that gurgled with fresh water, leading to a stream that fed finally into the river. He drove onto the carpet of whisper-soft pine needles, parking beneath the huge trees. Getting out of the car, he walked over to the cottage, climbed the steps up onto the porch, and sat down in a wooden rocker with a deer hide seat.

The wind soughed through the pines with that unmistakably high, strange, and yet comforting sound. Dylan closed his eyes and let memories flow over him like the spring breeze. He thought of picking blackberries with his grandmother and of the fresh-baked cobbler, sweet and tangy and rich with butter; swimming in the river with a half-wild, silver-and-black German shepherd named Hank, the undisputed king of the woods . . .

"Jesus is calling the weary to rest—
Calling today, calling today;
Bring him thy burden and thou shalt be blest;
He will not turn thee away."

The clear, sweet voice lifted in song was one Dylan had first heard more than a quarter of a century before, and the years had changed it not at all.

"Jesus is calling,
Is tenderly calling today."

Opening his eyes, Dylan saw her through the light-dappled screen of shrubs and saplings that lined the stream banks. She wore an old-fashioned bonnet tied beneath her chin, a faded print housedress, and black rubber boots three sizes too large for her. A slick willow branch strung with a half-dozen catfish lay across her shoulder, and a can of Lazy Ike fish bait was clutched in her thin brown fingers.

"Mattie."

She stopped, cocked her head to one side like a puppy hearing a strange noise, and peered into the glade beneath the pines. "Is dat you, Marbles?"

Dylan smiled, remembering how she had given him the nickname because she thought his eyes looked like two blue marbles. "It's me, all right."

She ambled across the culvert and across the thick blanket of pine needles, her faded brown eyes brightening with good will. "Well, now. Ain't you a sight." She set the fish and the can down next to her, gazing up at Dylan. Then she put her hands on her narrow hips. "You ought to be ashamed of yo'self. I guess you know dat already."

"Why's that, Mattie?"

Climbing the steps, she sat down on a church pew next to the front door. " 'Cause I ain't seed hide or hair of you in almost a whole year. Dat's why."

"I've been pretty busy."

"Ain't nobody dat busy." Mattie glanced around the place. "Where yo' folks at?"

"Visiting in New Orleans."

Shaking her head slowly, she made a clicking sound with her tongue. "Lawd a mercy! I don't see why people go down to dat wicked city. Sodom and Gomorrah ain't got nuttin' on dat place."

"Well, Susan has to see her folks, and she can't help where they live."

"I reckon dat's so."

"The food's good, too."

"Yeah, I 'spect dat bunch uh Sodomites was jes' sittin' down to a mess of shrimp Creole when de Good Lawd rained down His fire and brimstone, too." Mattie pushed out her chin in defense of her position. "Eatin' ain't no good enough reason to go down to dat terrible place."

Dylan laughed, remembering how he had always enjoyed being around Mattie. "You certainly have a . . . unique way of looking at the world, Mattie."

"Ain't but two ways, chile. Light and darkness. You either lookin' at it one way or t'other."

"I'm not sure I really understand what you're talking about, Mattie."

She looked intently into Dylan's eyes. "Don't you try to fool me, Marbles. You know 'xactly what Ise talkin' 'bout." Mattie jerked her birdlike head toward the front door of the cottage. "You was around de folks what lived in dis house too long not to know what Ise talkin' 'bout."

"You're right, Mattie," Dylan agreed reluctantly. "It's just that lately it seems like there's . . . well, a whole army of darkness coming at me."

"You muss be doin' somethin' right, den," Mattie said as though she already knew the script. "Hmmm, hmmm. The ol' Devil tryin' to mess wid you."

"I'm not sure I follow you."

"It mighty simple, chile. Folks ain't livin' right, he usually don't fool wid 'em much."

"Why not?"

"'Cause he already got 'em, das why. He jes' let 'em go ahead and mess up dey own lives."

Dylan gazed up at blue patches of sky showing through the leaves of the trees. "He's sure messin' with me, all right."

"You in good comp'ny, den. Ever last one of de disciples was whupped, stoned, put in de jailhouse. Dey finally kilt ever one of 'em, 'cept ol' John. And Paul"—Mattie took a red handkerchief from a dress pocket and wiped her forehead—"he was chained down in a dark hole 'til dey cut his head off."

Dylan glanced at Mattie's earnest face, the color of cream-lightened coffee beneath her floppy bonnet. "You really know how to cheer a fellow up, Mattie."

Her seamed lips curved back over her dentures, letting her tinkling laughter spill out. "I reckon I did lean kind of heavy on de bad side of things." Then she stared at the sunlight breaking green-gold in the leaves, and a gentle light filled her old eyes. "In spite of de trials, I wouldn't live no other way . . . not for no 'mount of money." She turned toward Dylan. "I 'spect Paul knew that better than anybody. He said, 'For I reckon dat the sufferings of dis present time are not worthy to be compared with de glory which shall be revealed in us.' "

Dylan found himself once again amazed by Mattie's knowledge of the Scriptures. She sometimes couldn't remember who the President was, had never read a newspaper, and watched only cartoons and *The Andy Griffith Show* on television, but could call up Bible verses like a Baptist deacon.

"What you gon' do about it?"

"It?" Dylan recalled that Mattie's remarks sometimes caromed like billiard balls, hitting him from unexpected angles.

"Yo' troubles."

"I've been thinking about that for the last day or two. I don't know where to start yet."

"Well, I do," Mattie said quickly, nodding toward the back of the cottage. "You git on out to yo' grampaw's office and ask God what to do. He'll help you." She gazed toward the mild blue sky. "There's enough prayers went up from out there, I 'spect de road to heaven's still paved wid 'em."

8

OUT OF THE DARK

Dylan walked with Mattie down the steps, across the yard and the culvert to the gravel drive. The wind sighed high in the pines; golden light flickered around them.

"Thanks for taking care of the old place, Mattie." Dylan looked back toward the cottage, secure in the shade and shelter of the big trees. "Maybe I'll move back out here one day."

Mattie merely nodded. Taking his hand in both of hers, she gazed into his eyes as though about to speak, then nodded again, picked up her fish and the bait can, and walked beneath the high, leafy canopy toward home.

Dylan watched Mattie until she became a faint, frail figure in the shadows, then went back to the house. Inside, he walked through all the rooms, allowing the voices of the past to talk to him, the faces to smile at him once again.

Going into the kitchen, he let the water in the sink run until the rusty brown color became clear, opened a vacuum tin, and made a pot of coffee. Pouring a cup and adding sugar, he took it with him out to the backyard, walking along the barely visible path to his grandfather's office, a small white frame building set at the edge of the woods between two ancient cedars.

Inside he breathed in the musty smell of old timbers, books, and papers, and the faint odor of pine oil. Sitting down at his grandfather's desk, he gazed at the faded photograph of a young couple in turn-of-the-century wedding dress.

He opened the middle drawer and took out his grandfather's Bible. Turning to Psalm 102, he read in a calm, quiet voice, " 'Hear my prayer, O LORD, and let my cry come unto thee. Hide not thy face from me in the day when I am in trouble; incline thine ear unto me: in the day when I call answer me speedily. For my days are consumed like smoke, and my bones are burned as a hearth. My heart is smitten, and withered like grass.' "

Closing the Bible, he placed his hands on its brown leather cover, worn smooth over the years in his grandfather's loving hands. It somehow gave him courage, knowing that a man like King David could have hard times the same as other people.

Dylan glanced at the picture of his grandparents again, remembering the time long ago when his fishing rod had been stolen and then lost in the river by a boy who lived down the road. Dylan had come to this same study to ask his grandfather what to do.

"That's easy. Pray for him."

Dylan was incensed. "Pray for him? But he stole my fishin' rod and then dropped it somewhere in the river. And all you can tell me is to pray for him?"

"It's not me telling you, anyway. It's what Jesus said we're supposed to do for our enemies; those who 'spitefully use us.' You don't like it, talk to Him about it."

Again Dylan stared at the picture. His grandfather's eyes seemed to see him once more, staring back through all the years since his death.

In a few minutes, Dylan said out loud, "All right, I'll pray for them . . . whoever they are." Kneeling next to the desk, he smiled at the picture. "But if it's all right with you, I'm going to pray for my family first."

In the purple dusk, Dylan left the office, went inside the

house, and opened a can of soup for supper. Then he went to the bedroom he had used as a boy and dropped off into a deep, dreamless sleep. Next morning, in the red glowing of sunrise, he was on the road to Baton Rouge.

———————

"Dylan, what a pleasant surprise!" Becky opened the door to her apartment. She wore a gray suit, white silk blouse, and a smile that was slightly off-center, as though she didn't know if it fit the occasion or not. "Come on in."

"I'd rather not." Dylan glanced inside, remembering the dazed and disoriented state he had awakened to in this apartment only a short time ago. "But I do need to talk to you."

"Sure. I was just on my way out." In the face of Dylan's stoic expression, her smile had slipped a half-inch. "Just let me get my purse."

Dylan waited for Becky on the landing and walked down to the parking lot with her.

"What's wrong, Dylan?" Becky fluffed her hair nervously. "Did something happen while I was in California?"

Ignoring her questions, Dylan took her by the arm and escorted her across the parking lot toward North Third Street. Threading his way through the early morning traffic, he led her along a concrete walk running beneath hundred-year-old live oaks dripping with Spanish moss.

A little breathless with their pace, Becky tried again, "Dylan, what's this all about?"

Offering her a seat on a stone bench commanding a direct view of the Capitol down a wide landscaped walkway, Dylan sat down next to her. "What happened that last night I saw you?" His voice sounded strained and harsh in his own ears.

Becky stared at him, a pained expression on her face. "Why are you treating me like this?"

A cold light gleamed in Dylan's eyes as he spoke. "Tell me what happened."

"Dylan, this isn't like you at all." She stood up. "When . . . whatever this is passes, call me."

Dylan grasped her arm just above the elbow, pulling her back down. "I'm not up to any games right now, Becky."

She rubbed her arm, her eyes bright with pain. "You, you hurt me."

Taking a deep breath, Dylan let it out slowly, fighting the red haze of anger before his eyes. Then in a controlled voice he told her what had happened to him. When he finished, he gave her a level stare and waited.

Becky's eyes widened. She placed her hand across her throat. "You think I had something to do with this?"

Dylan made no reply, not willing to adopt the part of inquisitor with Becky as his victim.

"Dylan, how could you think that I . . ." Tears suddenly flooded Becky's eyes, spilling down her cheeks. She placed her hands over her face.

Dylan took a white handkerchief from his inside coat pocket, handing it to her. When she had wiped her eyes and composed herself, he asked, "Just tell me what you remember about that night at the village, Becky."

"We had breakfast together." She took a compact from her purse, opened it, and began repairing her makeup. "Then you just got into your boat and left."

"That's it?"

Becky finished, gave the handkerchief back to Dylan, and put the compact away. "That's it. You said you were in a hurry to get home."

"I don't remember anything after that, Becky. For a while there I wasn't even sure if I had seen you that night, or if I was remembering that other time you had come out to the village when I was there. You think it's a coincidence that I ended up in your apartment?"

Becky stared at the azalea bushes lining the walkways. Their red and purple and white blossoms glowed in the sunlight. "I haven't the slightest idea."

"Who else has a key?"

"The buildings belong to the state. I'm sure there are other keys somewhere."

Dylan brooded over the legal walls that were slowly closing in on him and the likelihood that Becky was somehow involved in the conspiracy. *She could never do something like this. What reason would she have?*

"Are you all right, Dylan?"

Dylan stared at the Capitol building, its limestone walls gleaming in the morning sunshine. "No."

"Is there anything I can do?"

"Not that I can think of."

Becky placed her hand on his forearm. "Will you still work security for me?"

"I don't think that would be a good idea, Becky." He glanced at her, worry lines creasing her forehead. "Not under the circumstances."

She looked at him with pain-bright eyes. "You still think I'm involved . . . somehow."

Dylan thought back on their school years. He could almost hear her laughter as they walked home from school together; could almost smell the perfume she had worn at their senior prom. "No, I don't think that anymore."

"Thank goodness!" Becky sighed. "I'd hate to lose you after all these years."

"Lose me?"

"Your friendship, I mean, silly." Becky smiled and squeezed his arm. "You're the best friend I ever had."

"I've always liked you a lot, too, Becky." Dylan stood up, letting her hand fall away. "Well, I guess I'd better get busy and see if I can get myself out of this mess."

"Aren't the police working on it?"

Dylan nodded. "They're supposed to be, but clearing a cop

they think has turned bad isn't going to be at the top of their list of things to do."

———————

Through the window, Dylan could see the flat, green expanse of the drill field he had marched on as an ROTC cadet, and beyond it the massive stone bulk of Tiger Stadium. "Nice view you've got here, Wes."

"Yeah. It's the main reason I rented this place." Wes sat on the edge of his single bed, pulling his boots on. "I stand there sometimes and look out at the stadium." He sounded almost reverent as he continued. "I can almost believe that there's a game that night . . . and that I'm getting myself mentally ready for it."

Dylan turned away from the window. The view inside Wes's efficiency apartment wasn't so nice. The foot of the bed and both straight-backed chairs were draped with rumpled clothes. Tennis shoes and socks were scattered about the worn hardwood floor, and newspapers cluttered the small table next to the kitchenette. "I heard that *Southern Homes and Gardens* plans to do a spread on your apartment in their next issue."

Wes pushed his sleep-tousled hair back from his face and stood up. "Yep. They were planning to use Rosedown Plantation, then they saw my place." He glanced around the room. "Well, you can see why they changed their minds."

Dylan watched Wes head down the short hall to the bathroom. "You see Chet much?"

Wes's voice was accompanied by the sound of running water. "I'll be seeing him every week now. Vicki decided to move back to Baton Rouge. We usually made most of the ball games in the fall and went fishing in the spring and summer."

"It's hard to believe he's already twelve."

"Yep." Wes's words garbled around the toothbrush in his mouth. "Looks more like a fifteen-year-old, though. I think he's gonna be taller than I am."

Dylan piled the clothes from one chair onto the other and sat down. "I'll bet he's gonna be a humdinger of a football player in another three or four years."

Wes walked into the room, his hair wet and slicked down, his face washed clean of sleep. "He already is. Three or four of the high school coaches are trying to get his mother to move into their district so he can play for them." He grinned and poured two cups of coffee, handed one to Dylan, and sat down on the bed. "It's strictly against the rules, but then we know people don't always follow the rules, don't we?"

Dylan nodded slowly, staring at the dark, steaming coffee. "Looks like the only way I'm gonna get to the bottom of this fix I'm in is to break a few myself."

Wes leaned back on his elbows, eyes trained on Dylan over the rim of his cup as he spoke. "Elucidate."

"First of all, I don't have any legal authority, and second, it looks like it's gonna take some pretty drastic action to find out who's behind it."

"From what I gathered on the phone, you're gonna need a lot of help on this one. And that shot through the windshield of your boat wasn't an accident, if you ask me."

"Maybe not," Dylan conceded reluctantly. "Anyway, Emile and everybody else in our department is with me, but I'm afraid this is out of their league. I spent the whole morning trying to run down a lead on anybody who might have seen something the night it happened, but there's precious few people around the Pentagon that time of night."

"You bust any drug dealers in the last few years who might have a score to settle with you?"

Dylan quickly thumbed through the files in his head. "No heavy hitters. Just a few bush league players in the local area, mostly in Maurepas Parish. You never can tell, though. Sometimes a man can get a notion in his head over something that doesn't amount to much."

113

"There's always that ol' political grudge I talked to you about that day at the mansion."

Smiling ruefully, Dylan said, "I've never heard of a political grudge going this far."

Wes squinted over his cup. "Don't tell me you forgot about that sniper on the Capitol grounds. That wasn't but six, maybe seven years ago."

"That was a little more than politics, Wes. That was kidnapping children . . . and maybe murder." Dylan gazed out the window at the afternoon light casting long shadows across the campus. "Besides, I'm out of the mainstream down in Evangeline. I haven't had any political troubles in years."

"Hate has a long memory, son."

"Maybe you're right." Dylan sipped his coffee, frowned at the cup, and set it on the floor beside his chair. "I still think my best bet is to stick with the present, though." He shrugged. "The problem is I don't know what to do next."

"I do."

Dylan leaned forward in his chair, his eyes fixed on Wes. "You do?"

"Yep." An enigmatic grin crawled across his freckled face. "Ol' Wes always has a contingency plan."

"Let's have it, then."

"I'm getting together with one of my snitches. He's got a handle on most all the dealers in South Louisiana." Wes finished his coffee, got up, and put his cup in the sink. "If one of 'em is out to get you, he oughta know about it."

"When's this going down?"

"How's tonight sound?"

Dylan stared at a framed school picture of Chet on Wes's nightstand. Thinking of how much he missed Erin already, he was grateful that Wes would help him in the midst of his own troubles. "Fine. What're we doing till then?"

"You can stay here and catch some sleep. Looks like you could use it." He slicked the back of his long hair down with his hands. "I've got some pressing business with a little señorita who teaches in LSU's foreign language department. She thinks I'm mucho hombre."

"It's even cold here in April." Dylan zipped his light jacket and stepped farther back into the alcove out of the wind. Above him, the massive bulk of Tiger Stadium rose toward the midnight sky. "When I was in school out here, we used to say the north wind originated somewhere back in North Stadium."

"You turning into a pansy in your old age, Dylan?" Wes shoved a Camel between his lips, flicked a kitchen match into flame with his thumbnail, and lit the cigarette. In his black T-shirt and faded Levi's, he looked as though he had just stepped out of the black-and-white fifties classic *Blackboard Jungle*.

Dylan glanced at his friend faintly outlined by the street-lights. "Guess I'm just not a 'mucho hombre' like you, Wes."

Wes laughed, then took a draw on his cigarette, its tip glowing red in the near dark. "Don't make fun of me, son. I helped promote international relations with Latin America tonight. I'm even thinking about going into the diplomatic corps."

"Where's this mythical snitch of yours, Wes?"

"He oughta—"

At that moment Dylan heard the sound of running footsteps along the walkway next to the stadium.

Wes peered around the edge of the alcove. Reaching out, he grabbed a short, stocky man wearing shoulder-length hair and a denim jacket. "Here he is now. What's your hurry, Peaches? You're not running out on me, are you?"

The little man stared up at Wes from pale eyes, wide and fearful above his beard that grew almost to his eye sockets. "T-t-t-tiger!"

"Settle down, partner." Wes took Peaches by the shoulders and shook him. "Now, what's wrong?"

Having lost his ability to speak, Peaches stepped back from Wes and pointed frantically toward North Stadium Road.

Dylan peered out into the night. Walking down the center of the road toward the main campus, the five-hundred-pound Bengal tiger looked like an oversized house cat out for a midnight prowl around the neighborhood. Dylan turned his stunned expression back on Wes. "He's not lying. There's a tiger out there!"

Wes stepped to the edge of the alcove and looked, rubbed his eyes, and looked again. "It has to be Mike. He must have gotten out of his cage."

Leaning over, Dylan slipped the .38 Smith from its ankle holster, flicking the cylinder open to reassure himself that it held all five cartridges.

"I wouldn't shoot him with that peashooter. You'll only make him mad." Wes held his .357 in his big hand, its barrel pointing toward the high concrete ceiling.

"Fine with me. You stay here with your cannon, and I'll go get some help."

"Let me go, too," Peaches whispered, clutching at Dylan's arm. "I ain't even got a gun."

Dylan glanced at the terrified, short-legged man. "You'd be safer here with Wes."

"Where you goin'?" Wes kept his eyes trained on the tiger that continued his steady pace eastward.

"The campus security building's on the other side of the road at the bottom of the hill. If I can make it over there, they can call somebody."

"If that thing sees you, you're a dead man, Dylan."

Dylan glanced at the tiger. "That's true. You go. I'll stay here with Peaches."

"Bum knee," Wes said, tapping the side of his leg with his gun barrel.

Dylan watched the tiger edge over to a stand of pines growing near the stadium, sit down, and begin licking his left foreleg, then stretch out under the trees. "Looks like he's taking a break. Time to get going."

"Here, maybe you oughta take this." Wes held his big revolver toward Dylan.

Shaking his head, Dylan slipped the .38 Smith inside his belt at the small of his back. "I'll hang on to the one I'm used to. You just keep your eye on that monster, and if he comes at me, get there as quick as you can"—he glanced back at the tiger—"and don't be stingy with the bullets."

Keeping his eyes trained on the tiger, Dylan angled westward away from him toward the street and a grove of trees. When he was in the shadows, he waited until the animal's head was turned away from him, resting on its paws. Then he walked as quickly and as quietly as he could across North Stadium Road, finding thin shelter behind a row of crepe myrtles.

Walking obliquely away from the tiger, he headed east toward the squat lighted building that housed the campus security office. Just as he reached the cross street, opposite the office, a deafening roar split the night. Dylan froze, picturing the great gaping mouth of the tiger just behind him. When he forced himself to look, he saw that the big cat had sat up, its head lifted as the roar turned into a sleepy-looking yawn. Then it stood up, stretched lazily, and lay back down.

Dylan sprinted across the road and into the fluorescent glare of the office.

Seated behind a cluttered green desk, a slim, dark-haired woman in a uniform turned wide, fearful eyes on him. "Did you hear that?"

Dylan nodded. "Tiger." His brain seemed to be short-circuited, unable to furnish him with any other words.

"You mean Mike's loose?"

Dylan nodded again. Now he seemed to have lost the power of speech altogether.

The girl thumbed frantically through a faculty telephone book. "I've got to call the vet!"

"He's not sick. He's loose!"

"Here it is." Placing the tip of her forefinger on the page, she dialed the number. "He'll know what to do."

Dylan stared out the window at the tiger. Beyond and above it rose the massive bulk of the stadium. He picked out the niche that held Wes and Peaches but could see only the shadowy darkness. Five minutes later, two campus security units screeched to a halt in front of the office. The drivers kept their lights on, neither getting out of their cars.

Turning to the girl, Dylan said, "See if you can get them to make a little more noise, will you?"

"They're scared."

"I know the feeling." Dylan watched the tiger get to its feet, stare at the two cars in front of the office, then amble across the road and into the shadow of the trees.

At that moment a gray sedan pulled slowly alongside the two officers and stopped.

"That's Doc Grimes," the girl said. "He's always real calm. He'll know what to do." She stood up and walked to the door. "He got my cat out of a tree one time."

Dylan stared at the woman with an expression of disbelief, opened his mouth to speak, then pushed past her and out the door. "Doctor Grimes."

The vet, a bookish-looking man in his mid-thirties, turned toward Dylan. "I'm afraid I'm a little busy right now."

"I noticed earlier that the gate to Bernie Moore Stadium is open. Maybe we could drive him in there."

"Capital idea. I've got a pistol that shoots tranquilizer darts." Grimes grinned at Dylan. "Looks like our two stalwart campus security officers are chained inside their cars. You want to try and shoot a dart into our Fighting Tigers' mascot?"

"You're the doctor." Dylan could think of nothing at that moment that he would like to do less.

"So I am." He reached into his car and grabbed a shotgun off the front seat. "Know how to use this?"

Dylan nodded. He felt himself losing the power of speech again. Out in the darkness at the far edge of the light, he saw the tiger, standing still and looking back over its shoulder at the activity around the office.

Grimes barked some brief instructions to the officers, then he and Dylan got into his car. They bumped over the curb, driving slowly and directly at the tiger. The two officers flanked them slightly ahead.

Amazingly, the tiger, after a cursory growl, walked away, allowing itself to be channeled through the gate and out onto the infield of the track. Grimes drove through after him, got out, and closed the gate, then turned off his headlights and drove within fifty feet of the tiger.

Cutting his engine, Grimes said, "I've got to get three of these darts into him to put him down." He gazed at the tiger, now sprawled on the infield's cool spring grass. "Stay close and just behind me. If he charges, shoot for the head and get as many rounds off as you can."

Again Dylan nodded. He jacked a round into the chamber and punched the safety off. His throat felt as dry as a winter leaf. His heart pounded against his rib cage; blood roared in his ears.

Grimes got out, holding the pistol down at his side, and walked directly toward the tiger, which faced away from him at an angle. Dylan, the stock of the shotgun pressed against his shoulder, followed Grimes to his right and five feet behind him.

"This is it," Grimes whispered. He raised the pistol and fired, striking the animal's left flank. A thunderous roar erupted from the tiger as it leaped up, raking at its flank. Grimes, down on one knee, reloaded and fired again. The dart hit high on the shoulder. This time the animal bolted forty yards down-field, trying to get away from the stinging pain.

Grimes continued his approach, slow and cautious. Now the tiger turned toward him. It took three steps forward on wobbling legs. Stopping, it tried again, but fell over on its side, attempted to get up and fell back down.

Expelling his breath in a rush, Grimes walked closer and shot a final dart into the still struggling animal. Thirty seconds later the tiger lay still.

Grimes walked over, knelt down, and gave the tiger a quick once-over. "Let's see if we can get ahold of a pickup and get this beast back home."

Dylan looked across the infield. Wes, twenty yards in front of the two officers, walked toward them, his .357 pointing toward the ground.

"You boys got him corralled?" Wes glanced at the tiger, then back at Dylan.

"Doc Grimes did," Dylan answered. "I was just along for the fun of it. Why don't you go get your pickup and we'll haul this thing to his cage." He turned toward Grimes. "That sound all right to you, Doc?"

"Fine. Five of us ought to be able to handle him."

Resting the shotgun on his shoulder, Dylan walked over to Wes. "What happened to Peaches?"

Wes laughed. "He did pretty good until that last roar about five minutes ago. Then he lit out like a scalded dog." He turned to go get his pickup, then looked back as he walked away. "Don't worry. We'll catch up to him later. I know his hang-outs."

Grimes called out to the two officers, staring at the tiger as though he could leap to life at any second. "C'mon, boys. He's out for the count now."

Dylan laid the shotgun on the backseat of Grimes' sedan, then sat down on the car's fender. He glanced at Grimes, then gazed at the sleeping tiger.

Grimes sat down on the other fender. "It's an . . . interesting world, isn't it?"

"How's that, Doctor Grimes?"

"After our little experience together, I think you can call me Artie." Staring at the tiger, he said, "You never know what's going to come at you out of the dark."

9

THE HUSTLE

"Do we have to go to Redbone Alley?" Dylan sat next to Wes in his pickup. After taking the remainder of the night to chase down Peaches and discover that he could give them no useful information, Dylan wanted only a shower and a bed. "Besides, it's seven in the morning. What time do you think they get up over there?"

"I think some of 'em never go to bed." Wes, a Camel dangling from his lips, sneered at Dylan through the rising stream of blue-white smoke. "I remember the time we'd go nonstop for two, three days. Now, one all-nighter and you start whimpering on me."

"I'm a little out of practice." Dylan thought back on the nights he had spent on stakeout in the Bicentennial Burglar case. He had hoped that he could spend his nights in his own bed for a while after that, but it was not to be.

"Well, you stick around me for a while, partner. I'll get you back in shape again."

Dylan gazed out the window at the rush hour traffic on I–10. "I don't think I'm interested in getting back in shape for this kind of thing."

"If you want to get your family back together again, you better get serious about it."

"You're right. My brain's back in Evangeline, I guess." Dylan glanced at his old friend, knowing he must be thinking of his own lost family. "I appreciate your help in this, Wes. You and Emile are about the only cops I got in my corner."

Wes shook his head. "Nah. Most of 'em are on your side. They know a setup when they see one. They're just afraid of losing the things that I've already lost."

Dylan decided Wes would be better off if he avoided the subject of families. "I meant to ask you something last night, but our tiger chase kind of put it off."

"What's that."

"Peaches . . ."

"What about him?"

"How'd a drug dealer get a name like Peaches?"

Wes smiled and the burden of old sorrows seemed to lift a little. "So the story goes, when he was a kid he used to steal peaches from the neighborhood grocery. Loved 'em so much he just couldn't keep his hands off them."

Dylan pictured the furtive little man with his eyes full of fear. "He should have stuck with the peaches."

Wes took the exit ramp, turned left, driving beneath an overpass, then parked on the street. Dylan got out, walking with him underneath a trestle that took them into Redbone. The double row of shotgun houses, tin-roofed with remnants of imitation brick and tarpaper clinging to their sides, ran in a straight line from the railroad trestle to the woods.

Early sunlight glared down on discarded bicycle parts, scrap iron, broken toys, and treadless tires. A few scrawny chickens pecked about on the hardpan. Underneath the first house, a mangy red dog glared sullenly at them from the end of a rusty chain that was looped around a water pipe.

"Oh, not you agin!" A school bus seat on the front porch groaned under the weight of the woman who covered it from end to end. She wore a yellow satin housecoat and pink mules. "I thought I'd seed the end of you."

Wes turned his head, whispering to Dylan as they approached the woman. "Erline used to deal out of her house. We've got some charges we're holding in abeyance on her, so she graciously cooperates with us . . . sometimes."

"I remember her."

"What you whispering 'bout?" A red plastic radio on the windowsill behind her played "You'll Never Find Another Love Like Mine" by Lou Rawls.

Wes stopped at the bottom of the steps, his hands stuffed in the hip pockets of his Levi's. "Just commenting on your radiant beauty, Erline."

"I bet you was."

"Erline, this is—"

"Mr. Dylan St. John," Erline finished for him.

Grinning at Dylan, Wes said, "She remembers you, too. She's a sharp lady."

"I ain't got time for yo' jivin', Wes Kinchen. Git yo' b'iness over and git outta my face."

Wes turned a stonefaced expression on her, but it gradually cracked, turning into a smile. He threw back his head and laughed. "An honest woman. You gotta love her for that."

Erline turned her street-wise gaze on Dylan. "You got yo'-self in a mess of trouble."

"That I did, Erline. That I did." Dylan sat down on the edge of the porch, placing himself in a much lower position than Erline, in direct violation of the rule that ambitious civil servants and most politicians hold to.

"That's why we're here, Erline. We're counting on you to give us some help."

Erline shrugged her ponderous shoulders, and the yellow satin quivered down to the imitation leather she sat on. "I don't know who done it, if dat's whut you mean."

Wes stepped up onto the porch, sitting down in a rickety chrome-plated chair with red cushions. "You know something, Erline?"

Erline jutted her heavy chin at Wes, then turned to Dylan. "I know folks say you always treated 'em fair when you was a patrol officer, St. John."

"Nice to hear that," Dylan replied, wondering why *parole* was difficult to pronounce for so many people.

"You wouldn't a heard it if it wudn't what people tole me, St. John."

"Give me a name, Erline." Wes leaned forward in his chair, elbows propped on knees.

"I don't know who done it." She held Wes's gaze, her lips pressed into a thin line.

Wes spoke softly now, his voice coaxing, urging her. "Talk to me, Erline."

"I ain't much in the middle of things no mo'." Erline shook her head slowly. "Thank de Good Lawd fo' dat." She glanced at Wes, then at Dylan. "They's some new people in de drug b'iness now. I don't know who."

Dylan felt another stone wall facing him. "Anything you could tell us might help."

"Big shots."

"What does that mean?" Wes asked.

"I don't know. All I heared is some big shots was gettin' in on de drug money."

Dylan felt something rubbing his calf, looked down, and saw the red dog. Reaching down, he scratched a mange-free area of the animal's head. He heard the dog's tail thumping against a pillar beneath the house. "Anything else?"

Erline shrugged again. "De drugs come up through de swamps like dey allus did. Den somebody take 'em out de state and bring de money back."

"Sounds pretty ordinary to me," Wes said.

"Tole you I didn't know nuttin'."

"Except there's some big shots involved. What kind of big shots, Erline?"

"Dey all de same to me." She folded her hands over her

ample lap. "Big cars, shiny shoes, ever hair on dey head in place—you know de type."

"That's all?" Dylan asked, rubbing the dog's head, its tail drumming beneath the porch.

"Somebody in gov'mint."

"The government," Wes repeated. "Well, that cuts the number of suspects down to about eighty thousand . . . unless of course you count local and federal government, too."

"Das all I kin tell you."

"You've been a big help, Erline." Dylan gave the dog a final pat and stood up. "I appreciate your help."

Erline gave Wes a final scowl, then turned to Dylan. "I hope you gets out dis mess, Mr. Dylan St. John."

Dylan nodded a final thanks to Erline, then followed Wes out of Redbone Alley, underneath the trestle, and back to the truck. "What did you make out of what Erline told us?"

Wes dropped the tailgate of the pickup and sat down on it, his long legs touching the ground. "Somebody new in the drug trade. Somebody with some clout."

"You think they really work for the government?"

"Could be. There's so many people in Baton Rouge working in government, working for government, and connected to government that it doesn't really cut the possibilities much."

"What's our next move?" Dylan felt that he was sinking in a mire of confusion. His fear for Susan and Erin's safety, although there had been no threat directed toward them; the thought of being out of work and not able to support his family; and the charges he still had to face were driving him to the borders of despair. His thoughts seemed to swirl like leaves in autumn winds.

"Keep pushin' it." Wes set his jaw, his steely gaze on Dylan. "Don't give up on me now. We're gonna beat this rap and bring 'em to their knees."

Dylan found himself nodding again. He felt like some kind

of half-human puppet whose nodding string was being over-used by an insane puppeteer.

"Why don't you go home for a spell," Wes suggested. "See what's happening down in Evangeline. I'll be in touch with you in a day or two."

Dylan started to nod, then said, "All right." *See there, Dylan, you can still speak if you just put your mind to it.*

———

Evangeline lay quiet and restful on that troubled spring morning. Dylan parked his Volkswagen on the street and walked across the courthouse grounds in the sun-splashed shade of the old live oaks. All around him people went about their usual business, and he marveled for a moment that every-thing could remain on the same old course when his own life had taken such a drastic turn . . . yet he knew deep within him that his sense of isolation and loss was no unique experience. Taking a closer look at the townspeople, he wondered how many of them carried their hearts like stones inside their chests.

Entering the sheriff's office, Dylan greeted Elaine, Emile's secretary, with what he hoped was a cordial good morning. He found Emile poring over a stack of case files, his eyes slightly reddened, a gray-and-black stubble shadowing the lower por-tion of his weary-looking face.

"You need a shower and a night's sleep." Dylan poured a cup of coffee, then sat down on the heavy wooden chair at the side of Emile's desk.

Emile closed a manila folder, yawned and stretched, then leaned back in his chair. "I agree wholeheartedly, but I've got this renegade deputy that's keeping me from my bed."

"Making any progress?"

Shrugging, Emile scratched his stubbled chin. "Somebody with a grudge against you who's into drugs. These are the two threads I'm trying to pull together into one person." He yawned and stretched again. "It's a big job."

Dylan gave him the *Reader's Digest* version of what he had found out with Wes. "I've already told you about my talk with Becky. She says she doesn't know a thing about it."

"Maybe she doesn't." Emile held Dylan's steady gaze, then shook his head slightly. "You know her better than I do. Now this government angle. That might be something we need to take a closer look at."

"Where do we start?"

"The obvious place is with anybody in government you had a run-in with." A thought suddenly sparked in Emile's dark eyes. "I'm afraid that won't cull many, though."

Dylan thought back on his years in state government. "I didn't make that many enemies."

"Maybe not," Emile conceded.

"Nobody I can think of who would get involved in drug trafficking, anyway."

"You're probably right. Besides, you've been out of it for years now."

Dylan remembered Wes's words. *Hate has a long memory, son.* "Wes is going to check around and see what he can come up with."

"He's a good man. Got a lot of contacts, too . . . on both sides of the law." Emile stood up, walked over to the coffee service on a table next to the window, and poured a thick mug half full. After staring at a passerby on the sidewalk for a few seconds, he turned toward Dylan. "How's Susan taking this?"

Dylan held his cup in both hands, sipped the coffee, then placed the cup on the desk. "Phoned her a little while ago. Her mother thinks she should leave me for good."

Emile sat back down. "Why doesn't that surprise me? You're not paying any attention to what that woman says, I hope. I know Susan's got better sense."

Dylan remained silent, thinking back on the time when his work and his lack of judgment had almost gotten Susan killed by three bullets meant for him.

"Dylan, what's going on?"

Shoving the pain of that time away, Dylan said, "Nothing. Susan's handling it all right."

"You sure?"

Dylan nodded, thinking that nodding had become a prominent part of his communication system. *A nod's as good as a wink.* The words popped into his mind from nowhere. He almost said them out loud, then had to suppress a kind of insane laughter that was welling up inside him. "Yeah . . . I'm sure."

Emile leaned forward, resting his arms on his desk. "You're sure, but . . ."

"Maybe she's right."

"Maybe who's right?"

"Susan's mother."

"You mean about Susan's leaving you?"

Dylan stood up and began pacing the office. "Look at the trouble she's had in this marriage. Even after we got out of Baton Rouge, away from all that political claptrap, something's still coming back to haunt me . . . and it's dragging her into it." He stopped and stared at Emile. "Erin's five years old and I haven't even finished paying the hospital bill." He walked over and stared out the window. "She could pick somebody out of the telephone book and beat what she's got now."

"Hold on a minute." Emile got up and walked over to the door. "I'll be right back."

"Where you going?"

"Thought I'd go pick up some black balloons and a few sad records. If you're gonna have a pity party, we might as well do it up right."

Anger flared up inside Dylan. He spun around toward Emile, his hands doubling into fists.

"Now that's a good sign. You're getting mad." Emile went back to his desk. "I was afraid you were gonna cave in on me there for a little while."

Dylan took a deep breath, let it out slowly, and sat back

down next to the desk. He felt their friendship washing the anger away. "Thanks."

"Now, let's see if we can get you started in the right direction with what we already know so I can go home and sleep. Emmaline probably broke my supper dish by now."

On his way home, Dylan drove past Tony Fama's Mercantile. The cast of gray-haired regulars on the wide front porch, their numbers cut from five to three by time's wide and random scythe, waved from their rockers. The little black-and-tan feist no longer rose from his napping on the steps to bark at passing cars. He merely lifted his small head briefly, turned over, and went back to his doggy dreams.

Dylan parked in the shed, walked out to the dock, and sat down in the sunshine. He tried to collect his thoughts, put the few facts he had to work with into some logical order, but his brain was too muddled from lack of sleep and the urgency to pry himself out from under the boulder-like weight of his problems.

Finally, he went inside to shower and sleep. He sat down on the sofa for a moment to sort through the mail, and that was as far as he got. Dumping the letters and advertisements on the floor, he stretched out and fell into a restless sleep. The ringing of the telephone penetrated the ragged mists of his dreams. Willing himself to sit up, he opened his eyes to the sun's afterglow filling the room like a lavender mist.

In the kitchen, Dylan sat down on a stool next to the stove and picked up the telephone. "Yeah."

"You sound like the night shift at the mortuary."

"Wes. . . . What's going on?"

"Party at the Governor's Mansion."

Dylan rubbed his eyes with his free hand. "I'm married. You'll have to ask somebody else."

"Cute, Dylan. But at least you haven't lost what passes for your sense of humor."

"Thanks, Wes." Dylan felt a sudden sense of sadness and loss that made him physically weak. Fighting against it, he said, "What's really on your mind?"

"The party. We're not invited, but I know how we can find out what's going on."

"Why do we want to know?"

"I'm tired of this telephone talk. Just put on some dark clothes and get on up here to my place."

Dylan felt only half-awake. His chest held a dull pain like the aching of an old wound. "Dark clothes? I don't get it. You mean like something—"

"Stick your head in a bucket of water, will you?" Wes cut him off. "I feel like I'm talking to a first grader. Then put on something black and be here in an hour."

"All right." Dylan listened to the dial tone for a few seconds, then went back to the bedroom and put on a pair of Levi's and a black shirt.

The sound of a local band playing Van McCoy's disco anthem "The Hustle" carried across the water. Dylan stood next to Wes on the bank of Capitol Lake across from the Governor's Mansion. Above them cloud cover obscured most of the sky.

"You really think we oughta do this?"

Wes started walking around the lake toward the bright lights at the rear of the mansion. "This is something I want to see for myself. Maybe it won't amount to anything, but my buddy doing mansion security says we ought to take a look."

"How's he know what we're looking for?" Dylan caught up to Wes and walked along next to him. Frogs along the bank chanted their rain song.

"I told you I was gonna put out feelers everywhere I could think of." Wes stepped into a hole, twisting his bad knee. He muttered something to himself and continued, favoring the leg more than usual.

"You all right?"

Wes grunted. "Let's cut the gab unless we got something to say. I don't want to bring some green recruit in security down on our heads." He skirted an area lighted faintly by the arc lights at the back of the mansion. "Might be hard to explain an undercover state police officer lurking around the mansion with a suspended Maurepas detective."

Dylan followed Wes into a wooded area, pushing his way through the underbrush. Leaves lay sodden on the muddy ground; vines grabbed at them; an occasional fallen limb cracked beneath their boots.

Reaching the edge of the woods, Wes lay down on the damp ground and took his binoculars out of the carrying case. After a cursory look, he handed them to Dylan and said, "Looks like that's the place where the elite meet, all right."

Dylan held the glasses to his eyes, trained them on the mansion's back patio and garden area, and turned the focus ring until the image sharpened. Women in party dresses and men in three-piece, pastel-colored suits with open-collared shirts danced to yet another playing of "The Hustle." He recognized senators and state representatives, local power brokers, TV personalities, and even one Hollywood starlet.

"Well, what do you think?"

Dylan handed the glasses back to Wes. "I think that's a place I'd like to keep as far away from as possible."

"That's 'cause you got no class, redneck." Wes snorted. "Everybody wants to run with that crowd."

Staring out at the glare and glitter of the party, Dylan said in a hushed undertone, " '. . . he was everything to make us wish that we were in his place.' "

"What's that?"

"Just something I remembered from an old poem." Dylan yawned and rubbed the back of his neck. "You gonna tell me why you brought me out here now?"

Wes peered through the binoculars. "Nope."

"But you said—"

"I'm gonna show you." He handed the glasses to Dylan. "There's your answer, right now. Look to the left of the band, walking toward the buffet."

Dylan brought the glasses to bear on the spot Wes had described. She looked lovely in her long, peach-colored dress, wearing her hair in an elegant, upswept fashion. The man whose arm she held on to was tall, blond, and impeccably dressed in a black-tailored tuxedo. The last time Dylan had seen him, he was sweat-drenched and breathing heavily, trudging dejectedly off a tennis court. "Ralph Rayburn!"

"I thought you'd enjoy this."

Dylan laid the glasses aside. "What's he doing with Becky?"

"That, so the saying goes," Wes replied, "is the rub. What do your ol' ex-girlfriend and Baton Rouge's answer to George Hamilton have in common?"

"You still think Hamilton dated Lynda Bird Johnson to get out of the draft, don't you?"

"I know he did. And Rayburn's the same type," Wes said vehemently. "He just uses different methods and different people for his own purposes."

"Why Becky, then? She doesn't have any clout in this town"—Dylan glanced at the party—"that I know of. She's been out of state for years."

"Maybe they're just gettin' chummy."

"But Rayburn's married."

Wes gave Dylan a look of disbelief. "Well, perish the thought, then."

Dylan brushed Wes's comment aside. "Why did your friend at the mansion want me to see this?"

"Guess he thought you might put something together if you had enough pieces."

"I don't get the connection."

"Well," Wes said thoughtfully, "Rayburn never was especially fond of you, as I recollect."

"I beat him in a tennis match," Dylan explained, "but that was years ago." Then he reconsidered. "There was that business about the Y.O.U.R. program that turned out to be nothing but a sham for kidnapping children, but Ike and Donaldson took the fall for that. Rayburn got off scot-free."

"Well, maybe there's nothing to it, then. I doubt he'd go to all this trouble 'cause you beat him in a sissy tennis game."

Dylan ignored the barb Wes threw at his sport. Picking up the glasses, he trained them on Becky and Rayburn. After a few seconds, he laid them aside and said, "I'm going to make a call on Becky, anyway. Maybe it's just coincidence, her being with Rayburn, but I still want her to explain it."

"Now you're talking." Wes stood up, brushing off his clothes. "Why don't we—"

"Hold it right there, you two!"

Dylan stared into the beam of light that flashed on them, half-blinded by its brightness. He saw the dim outline of a uniformed figure, a heavy revolver in his hand.

"Git that light out of my face, Sonny!"

"Mr. Wes," the youthful voice replied. "Sorry, I thought y'all was some kind of perpetrators." The light went out and the pistol was holstered.

"Perpetrators, huh? You learn that word in your classwork at the academy, Sonny?"

"Uh, yessir." Sonny gave Dylan a suspicious glance. "What's he doing with you?"

"This is, uh, Roscoe Rice. He's just a deputy from out of town. I'm giving him a lesson in night surveillance."

"Oh. Well, I better git on back to my rounds. See you later, Mr. Wes."

"Sure thing. By the way."

"Yessir."

"You're doing a good job."

"Thanks. That means a lot coming from you."

Dylan watched the young man continue on around the edge of the woods, occasionally flicking his beam of light out into the darkness, then shutting it off after a second or two. Then he turned to Wes. "Roscoe Rice?"

"Think *you* could come up with a better name under the circumstances?"

"I guess not." Dylan fell in beside Wes as they headed back toward the lake, taking the open route around the woods now. A slow rain began, ticking on the leaves and dimpling the surface of the lake. "Guess it's not our night."

Wes glanced up at the black sky. "I think it's just not my century."

10

THE TEA PARTY

"Mama, if I ask you something"—Erin turned her sad blue eyes toward Susan—"you won't get mad at me, will you?"

Susan sat in a cushioned wicker rocker on the wide stone porch overlooking St. Charles Avenue. "Of course not, sweetheart. What's bothering you?"

"It's Grandma."

"Oh goodness! What's she done now?" Susan asked, her eyes wide in mock fright. "Has she threatened to sell you to that old wicked witch again?"

Erin giggled, the tapered fingers of her left hand held in front of her mouth. "No, ma'am. She didn't do that."

"Well, just what did she do?" Susan brushed a piece of lint from her linen skirt.

Erin frowned slightly. "Why don't she like Daddy?"

"Doesn't, Erin."

"Why doesn't she, then?"

Susan got up and walked over to the settee, sitting down beside her daughter. "She does like him, Erin. What makes you think otherwise?"

Shaking her head slowly back and forth, Erin repeated, "No, she doesn't like him," pronouncing her words slowly and distinctly. "She really doesn't."

"Why do you think that?"

Erin smoothed her ruffled dress and clasped her hands together in her lap. "She told me she wants us"—she glanced toward the front door as though someone might be spying on her through its leaded glass—"to come live down here with her."

"Oh, I think that's just her way of telling you how much she loves you," Susan explained, a little guiltily. "So much that she wants you to be with her all the time."

Erin shook her head again. "No, she really doesn't like Daddy." She turned her earnest face up toward Susan. "But I think he's a good daddy."

Susan put her arm around her daughter. "He is, Erin. He's the best daddy a little girl could have."

Erin climbed into Susan's lap. "We won't ever leave him . . . will we?"

"Not till billy goats wear frock coats"—Susan grinned—"or dogs and cats wear tall silk hats."

Erin giggled again, snuggling against her mother's breast. "I love you, Mama."

"I love you too, sugar." Susan put her arms around Erin, holding her close. She thought of all the times she had defended Dylan against her mother, especially in the past few days. She had been against their marriage from the beginning and seized every opportunity to try to prove she had been right in wanting Susan not to marry "that awful, uncouth, redneck Marine." She had made the word *Marine* sound like something that had to be picked up with rubber gloves or a shovel.

"Mama."

Susan leaped out of her thoughts, letting Erin unfold from her arms. "Yes, sugar."

"Can we go somewhere?"

"You tired of hanging around this big ol' house?"

Erin nodded.

Susan gazed out at the neutral ground on St. Charles. An

old iron streetcar rocking along its tracks whined to a stop at the intersection. Passengers began climbing down the steps, passing a short line of people waiting to get on board. "If we hurry, I think we can make it."

"We're gonna ride the trolley?"

"You bet!" Susan took her hand, bounding down the steps and the front walk toward the streetcar painted green and tethered to the power line above it. "Hold on, we're coming as fast as we can!" she yelled.

"Oh boy!" Erin squealed, her feet barely touching the ground as she held to her mother's hand. "This is fun!"

———

"She reminds me so much of Dylan." Helen St. John wore a beige cotton dress printed with tiny blue-and-white flowers. She stood at her kitchen door gazing through the screen at Erin, playing on the brick patio.

"Me, too," Susan agreed, "but I can't really say why. Everyone says she looks like me."

"Oh, she surely does." Helen turned reluctantly away from her only grandchild, sitting down at the table across from Susan. "The only feature that looks like Dylan are those blue eyes, and they're absolutely identical to his. It's just something in the way she moves and that certain light in her eyes when she gets really interested in something."

"She's a daddy's girl, I can tell you that."

Helen's dark eyes held a gentle light as she spoke. "I sometimes stand by the door when I'm alone and just pretend she's out there playing. Isn't that silly?"

Reaching across the table, Susan placed her hand on Helen's. "Not at all." She noticed that her mother-in-law had lost weight since she had last seen her. The delicate skin below her eyes held slight dark smudges as though she carried around an undefined weariness. "But anytime you get lonesome for your granddaughter, call us and we'll be right down to get you."

"I wouldn't want to bother you." Helen sipped her tea and took a tiny bite of a sugar cookie.

"You should spend more time with us, anyway," Susan insisted. "It's so peaceful and quiet out there on the bayou. We'd love to have you anytime."

"Maybe I'll do that." Helen smiled, the light in her eyes growing even softer. "You have fishing poles?"

"Loads."

"I could teach Erin how to fish. My grandmother taught me when I was just about her age."

Susan didn't tell her that Dylan had been taking Erin fishing with him since she turned three. "I'm sure she'd just love that. Why don't you ride back with us when we go home? Dylan will be tickled to death to see you."

"When do you plan to go?"

Susan had wondered why Helen had avoided the subject of Dylan's facing criminal charges. Not once had she mentioned it since their arrival. Now she felt that the time had come to clear the air. "Dylan's going to let us know when he's . . . resolved the problems up there."

Helen got up and walked over to the door, staring out at her granddaughter.

"Helen, are you aware of the trouble Dylan's in?"

She turned to face Susan, her eyes growing dark with sorrow. "I don't read the newspapers much."

"Then you really don't know?"

"Oh yes." Helen sighed, returning to her chair. "One of my neighbors was kind enough to point it out to me."

"I hope you don't think—"

"That Dylan was involved in something like that," Helen interrupted. "I raised him, Susan."

"All he has—"

"Susan!"

Susan was startled at the force of Helen's voice. Noticing the sparks of anger in Helen's eyes, she felt for the first time ever the sting of her disapproval.

"I'm sorry. Forgive me," Helen said immediately. "I'm not mad at you. It's just . . . just that I can't bear to discuss this. I don't want to even think about it."

"Yes, ma'am," Susan said. "I understand. But be assured, Dylan will see his way through this."

Helen nodded. "Yes, I'm sure he will." She walked back to the door. "I really should go get some things at the grocery." She turned around. "You are staying for supper?"

"Surely." Susan smiled. "Tell you what. You make me a list, and I'll go to the store for you. Then you can spend some time with Erin, just the two of you together."

Helen beamed at her daughter-in-law. "I think that would be lovely." She walked back to the table, sat down, and took Susan's hand. "I truly am sorry for speaking unkindly to you, Susan. You're such a wonderful wife for Dylan."

Susan squeezed Helen's hand in reply.

"It's just that," Helen continued, her voice breaking slightly, "that since Noah . . . since I lost him, I don't seem to have the strength to face up to things like I did when he was here. I guess I relied on *his* strength too much."

"Well, you've got Dylan and me now," Susan assured her, "and Erin, of course."

A smile lighted the shadows of Helen's face. "Yes, I do, don't I?"

"You're Mister Susslin, aren't you?"

Susslin opened the display case next to the counter and began filling it with pastries from his metal cart. "Yep. I don't believe I've had the pleasure."

"I'm Susan St. John, Dylan's wife." She laid her purse on the counter and held her hand out.

Susslin wiped his big hand on his white apron and took Susan's hand. "Pleased to meet you. I fed that husband of yours

a boxcar load of my pastries while he was going to school here."
He aligned the last doughnut in its proper place, then slid the
glass door shut. "That Dylan was a cutter. I can tell you that."

"He still is," Susan grinned.

Susslin laughed. "I'll bet he is." Pushing the cart through
the swinging doors into the kitchen, he returned to the
counter. "You know, he was in here not long ago. Him and
that Burke girl come in at almost the same time after all these
years. That's some coincidence, huh?" He pointed to a table
next to the window. "Sat right there where they always did
when they was sweethearts here at school."

Dylan had told her about his "chance" meeting with
Becky, but hearing it from somebody else in the place where
it had happened caused an aching in her chest, which turned
suddenly into hot anger. "Yes, Dylan told me about seeing
her."

"I always thought them two would get married someday."
Susslin's eyes held a faraway look as though he had returned to
those years he spoke of. "Funny how things never work out
like you think they will."

"Yes, it is." Susan took a deep breath, letting her anger flow
out with her expelled breath. *This is nonsense to be jealous of
something that happened so long ago when Dylan was just a boy.*
Then an image of him in Becky's bed flashed unbidden before
her eyes. She knew in her heart that Dylan had told her the
truth about what had happened to him, but the image continued flickering to life around the shadowy edges of her mind.

"What can I get for you, ma'am?"

Susslin's deep voice jerked Susan away from her nightmar-
ish vision. "Dylan always bragged on your apple fritters. And
a cup of coffee, please."

"Best in New Orleans." Susslin set the warm pastry on a
white saucer and filled a thick mug with coffee. "Here you go."
He held an upturned palm toward Susan's dollar bill. "No. It's
on the house. You're a first-time customer. Besides, I made so

much money off your husband them years he was coming in here, I oughta give him part ownership."

Susan thanked Susslin, found an empty table next to the plate glass window, and sat down. Then she realized it was the same table Susslin had pointed out as being Dylan and Becky's. She almost got up and took another table but decided that she was not giving in to petty jealousies and foolish notions.

Pouring cream into her coffee, Susan noticed a man only two or three inches taller than her, standing next to a table gazing out at the uniformed teenagers in the schoolyard across the street. He had dark, wavy hair and wore a navy pinstriped suit with a red tie. *Joe. That can't be Joe Loria. I do believe it is.*

At that moment, the man turned toward her as though he had heard her thoughts. His brows lifted, eyes twinkling with merriment as he walked briskly over to Susan's table. "Susan. I can't believe it's really you!"

"Joe. So good to see you." She held her hand out, but Loria had already leaned over, put his arm around her shoulders, and kissed her on the cheek.

"Mind if I sit with you?" Loria asked, but he had already gone to get his coffee before Susan could answer. Returning and sitting down in the chair next to her, he leaned back and admired her openly. "You're prettier than you were when we were in school together. I'll bet you don't remember how I used to ask you out almost every week."

Susan slid her chair a few inches away from him. "You always did have a ready compliment, Joe."

Loria's face grew serious. "You never did go."

"Go where?"

"Go out with me. Why was that?"

Susan shrugged. "I really don't know. We always had fun together in class."

"Well, you didn't," Loria said, his eyes once again crinkling with his smile. "And now, here we are together after all these years, just like we're on a real date."

Scraping her chair a few inches farther toward the window, Susan said, "I don't think I'd go that far."

Ignoring her, Loria said, "What's an uptown girl like you doing over here on the Westbank?"

"Visiting my mother-in-law." Susan filled her sentences with settled-down-and-married allusions. "Our five-year-old daughter is with her now."

"Why're you here in this little bakery?"

"My husband always spoke fondly of this place. I just wanted to see what it looked like."

"He went to school at Holy Name?"

Susan nodded, feeling Loria's hand pressing against her forearm.

Loria looked out at the old brick school building across the street from the ancient Gothic church. "Not much of a school."

"Big enough for him to be city champion in tennis."

"Tennis, huh." Loria's upper lip curled back in a sneer. "That's kind of a sissy sport."

Susan sipped her coffee, refusing to be baited by Joe's comments. "And how's *your* life going, Joe?"

"Great! Just great!" He fished a business card out of his inside pocket, handing it to Susan. "I live over here in Gretna, now. All the action's on the Westbank. Twelve years in the insurance business and I have my own company."

"I'm glad to hear you've made a success of your life. You always were a nice boy."

Loria leaned back in his chair. "I'm not a boy anymore, Susan. I'm a grown man now." He gazed directly into her eyes. "I drive a car, buy my own clothes. I can even eat shrimp Creole without dripping the sauce on my shirt."

Susan smiled, running her fingertip around the rim of her mug. "Next thing you'll tell me you're a father."

"Nope. Never got married." Loria gave her a crooked smile. "And it's your fault."

"My fault? That makes absolutely no sense whatsoever, Joe Loria."

"I think you ruined me for other women."

"What do you mean I *ruined* you?" Susan said, slapping him playfully on the arm. "I never even dated you."

"I think that's probably the reason."

Susan shook her head. "You're still not making any sense. It's just like we were in school again."

"Makes perfect sense to me," Loria explained. He gazed out at the towering stone facade of the church. "I always had this dream of what you'd be like"—he glanced at her—"you know, if we were actually . . . together . . . on a date. Well, it never happened, so I've been stuck in this fantasy all these years."

"No wonder you're so successful in the insurance business. I'll bet you could sell fur coats in Tahiti."

"Hey, that's an idea," Loria said, snapping his fingers. "I could corner the market in no time." He finished his coffee. "So, what do you think?"

"I think you're just as nutty as you always were." Susan began to feel relaxed and at ease. It was almost as though she had left the worries and responsibilities of being a wife behind her.

"No, I mean what do you really think about my holding on to this fantasy all these years?"

Susan noticed the fragrance of Loria's cologne. "First of all, I think you're a little naïve if you expect me to believe that line of yours." But inwardly she felt flattered at the thought of someone placing her on such a pedestal, even if the pedestal was constructed only of pretty words.

"But it's true," Loria insisted, taking Susan's hand. "Every woman I went out with was a disappointment. I kept comparing them to you."

"I have to leave, Joe." She pulled her hand away, pushing her chair back to stand up.

"I'm sorry." Loria turned a remorseful expression on her. "You're right. I was just using a line on you. Kind of." He let his breath out in a rush. "Comes with the business, I guess." Glancing at her, his face shadowed by a true or imagined sorrow, he said, "Fact is, I'm divorced . . . twice."

Noticing the sadness in Loria's eyes, Susan relaxed and remained seated.

Loria crossed his heart with his left hand. "It's true, though, that I've thought of you a lot over the years." He held his hand palm outward as though warding off an expected blow. "Now don't get mad. I've always considered you as someone very special in my life."

Susan nodded her head slowly. "Well, I guess it's all right for you to say that, Joe." She almost told him good-bye at that point, but a voice seemed to whisper to her that she was doing nothing wrong; that this man was merely an old friend from her childhood whom she was sharing a few memories with. *Besides*, she thought, *with that sad expression, he looks a little like Al Pacino.*

"Whew!" Loria grinned, the crinkle coming back to his eyes. "I really bared my soul to you that time. I hope you aren't embarrassed."

"Not at all." Susan thought of their school years together; the absolute freedom and lack of responsibility; no worries about bills to pay, and those long, indolent summer days that seemed they would never end.

Loria clasped her hand. "Why don't we go somewhere and get some real food. It's close enough to lunchtime." He glanced at his diamond-studded watch. "There's this little bar and restaurant I know that's got the best seafood gumbo in New Orleans."

Susan felt the same prodding as though someone were encouraging her to go, telling her it was perfectly all right to spend some time with an old friend. "I'd better not."

"Why?"

Smiling, Susan said the first thing that popped into her head. "Because I could never live up to that fantasy you've had about me all these years, Joe."

"You already have, Susan," Loria said, his voice sounding a little hoarse. "Besides, I play there on weekends, so they'll give us special treatment."

"You still play music?"

"Yep. Can't get that ol' trumpet-playing out of my blood." Loria squeezed her hand. "C'mon, whadda you say? It'll be a lot of fun. We can talk about the good ol' days."

"I don't know, Joe. I've got this shopping to do . . . Erin's at my mother-in-law's."

Loria turned on his Al Pacino look. "Aw, c'mon. We'll be back before you know it."

"Well . . ."

"Now, are you sure this child's old enough to drink tea?" Helen sat in a wrought-iron chair across the table from Erin. A child's tea service was arranged between them.

"Yes, ma'am." Erin placed a cup and saucer before her doll, seated in a toy high chair. "She's a very good baby, and I'll make sure she doesn't spill any and burn herself."

"Very well, then," Helen replied, pouring the imaginary tea from a flowered teapot. "And do you think she'd enjoy some of these sugar cookies?"

"Oh yes, ma'am! She just loves them!" Erin took the saucer from her grandmother, placing it in front of her doll. "Mama likes them, too. When's she coming home?"

"Oh, anytime now, I suppose," Helen replied, holding the tiny cup to her lips. "She's probably having to fight one of those long check-out lines at Schwegmanns."

Susan felt her face burning with shame as she stood at the screen door, gazing at Erin and Helen. Then she turned and began putting the groceries away. Stacking canned goods in the

147

pantry, she could hear the lilting music of her daughter's laughter. When she had finished, she joined them at the table and listened to Helen's soft, clear voice as she sang Erin's favorite song:

"Jesus loves me this I know,
For the Bible tells me so."

Susan had a sudden glimpse of her wedding day and of Dylan slipping the plain gold ring on her finger. *How could I even think of going somewhere with Joe Loria, or any other man? What's wrong with me? Oh, Dylan, I miss you so much! Please bring us back home soon.*

PART THREE

———

HELEN

11

FADING GLORY

Dylan stood in front of the massive stone staircase of the main entrance to the Capitol building. Behind him, on its white pedestal, the statue of Huey P. Long surveyed the crowd entering and leaving and milling about the 450-foot-tall limestone structure. Long had built it so that "Every Man a King" would be something more than his political slogan. Every Louisianan could boast that his was the tallest state Capitol in the nation.

With the legislature in session, Dylan had to park on a side street four blocks away and walk the old broken sidewalks past turn-of-the-century cottages and the stately 1840s mansions of Spanish Town. The azaleas and flower gardens had burst forth with color. In the cool, scented morning air, he thought of Susan and Erin and of how the three of them had always enjoyed their outings on these few perfect spring day, hemmed in by winter's cold rains and summer's sultry nights and blistering days. Now he was alone in the best of weather.

Then he saw her, crossing the street from the Pentagon and walking briskly along the sidewalks of the formal gardens toward the Capitol. He crossed Capitol Drive and took a walkway that intersected her route.

"Dylan. What a nice surprise!" Becky looked the picture

of a young businesswoman in her charcoal-colored suit and white silk blouse.

In the face of Becky's professionalism, Dylan felt like country-come-to-town in his boots and jeans and faded denim shirt. "You look like you're in a hurry. Got an appointment over at the Capitol?"

Becky gave him a puzzled frown. "Why, yes, I do. Does that meet with your approval?"

"Somehow"—Dylan watched her expression change, small lights dancing in her eyes—"I think my approval doesn't play any part in your decision-making process."

Becky folded her arms across her chest defensively. "Are you practicing to be the villain in your school play, Dylan? Because I simply don't have the time to play the part of the accommodating victim."

Dylan gazed at this woman he had known as a girl. Fuming with righteous indignation, she reminded him again of Scarlett O'Hara, this time facing down Rhett Butler. "Maybe I came on a little too strong, Becky."

Her face softened, and the sparks in her eyes died away. "Well, that's a little better." She unfolded her arms and stepped closer. "I don't see why you're so dead set on casting me as the bad girl, Dylan. It seems like every time you have a bad day, I'm the one you look for."

"It's not exactly like that, Becky. You have to admit that you were the last person I saw before my arrest and—"

"Not quite accurate," Becky cut him off. "The last person you *remember* seeing."

"Point taken," Dylan said, continuing his statement, "and it was your bed they found me in."

"I admit that much." Becky glanced at the grand staircase of the Capitol, crowded with the players and the watchers of Louisiana's political arena. "But you can hardly blame me because my bed was kind enough to take you in."

Dylan almost smiled at that one, then remembered Becky

and Ralph at the governor's party. "Do you mind if I ask you one simple question, Becky?"

"Well, I guess it's all right. At least I don't have to sit on a hard chair with bright lights in my face."

"Am I really coming on that strong?"

"Maybe it's the duration." Becky let her breath out in a whispering sigh. "I thought we had all this cleared up the last time you interrogated me."

Dylan let the thrust at his questions slide by. "Ralph Rayburn was, or maybe I should say *is*, someone who"—he gazed into her eyes—"let's just say, doesn't think kindly of me."

"So . . ."

"So you were getting awfully chummy with him at the governor's party."

"You were there?" Becky looked incredulous, caught off guard.

"Let's just say I saw the two of you together."

"You've got me dead to rights, Sheriff Dylan." She turned around, holding her wrists together at her back. "Put the cuffs on and take me to the calaboose."

Dylan was sure Becky was trying to avoid having to explain her closeness to Rayburn. "I think you've spent too much time with the Hollywood crowd, Becky."

She whirled around, dark eyes suddenly burning in her bright face. "And I think you've spent too much time in the company of dope pushers and street thugs! You think everybody is trying to hide something; that everybody's a crook; that nobody tells the truth. Don't you trust *anybody*, Dylan?"

Dylan felt the sting of her words but managed to let them bounce off. "Humor me, will you? I'd still like to know why you're so chummy with Rayburn."

Becky folded her arms again and gave him a cold stare. "Because he's the head of the Louisiana Tourist Commission, Dylan. And they're the people I'm working with to get this village completed so we can make a movie down here." She lost that first hard rush, then seemed to wilt like a ship's canvas in dead calm. "But then you already knew that."

"I didn't know Rayburn was heading up the tourist commission, Becky. I really didn't."

"You live here, Dylan," Becky reminded him. "How could you not know?"

Dylan rubbed the back of his neck, watched a fox squirrel peering from behind the trunk of a live oak, and found himself feeling a little foolish. "Do you have any idea how many political appointments there are to all the various commissions and boards and agencies in state government?"

"Well . . . no," Becky admitted.

"The governor alone makes about two thousand. You expect me to keep up with every political hack who comes out of the woodwork with a new administration?"

"Ralph's not a political hack. He's a true gentleman in the old southern tradition."

"Sure, Becky. And Ted Kennedy is president of the Richard Nixon Fan Club."

Becky glared at him, then whirled away and started down the sidewalk.

Dylan caught up with her, taking her by the arm. "I'm sorry, Becky. There's no sense taking my troubles out on you." She stopped but looked away from him. "It's just that I have information that someone's out to settle an old political score with me and—"

"And you think Ralph's the one," she interrupted him, turning around, hands on her hips.

"He's the only prospect I've got."

"What's he got against you?"

Dylan filled her in on the political vendetta report he had gotten, omitting the informant's name and position. "So that's about the whole picture."

Becky shook her head in disbelief. "Dylan, you said this all happened seven years ago. Do you really think someone could carry a grudge that long, especially since he wasn't even involved in the plot or crime or whatever it was?"

"I didn't say he wasn't involved, Becky. I said that he wasn't charged with anything."

"That's good enough for me."

Dylan felt all he was accomplishing was to further alienate an old friend. "I guess I should apologize for coming down so hard on you, Becky. I didn't plan to, it's just that . . ." He let the words hang in the air, disgusted by his own inability to pull his family and himself out of the trouble that seemed to somehow be of his own making. And it looked as though Ralph's role as the prime suspect was proving to be nothing but another dead end. *But who could it be . . . and what did I do to them?*

"You don't have to apologize, Dylan. I'm an old friend, remember? It'll take more than a few harsh words from you to change that."

Dylan didn't remember that his words had been all that harsh, but he said nothing. "I guess what's really getting to me is not having Susan and Erin around. It's like they've been sent into exile."

"At least she has someone like you to take care of her. Someone to love her."

Becky's words were soft, but Dylan saw for an instant the hard glitter in her eyes. "You can't blame yourself because you had a crazy husband, Becky. You just made a bad choice, that's all. You've got the rest—"

"I don't want to talk about that!" Becky almost shouted. "Besides, it's none of your business!"

Caught off guard by Becky's mercurial temperament, Dylan merely replied, "You're right."

"Oh, I don't really mean that," Becky moaned, pushing her hair back from her eyes with one hand. She kept her palm pressed against her forehead as she continued. "You've been so much help"—her haunted eyes turned on Dylan for just a moment—"and you saved my life. I don't know *what* I mean anymore." She struck at an imaginary enemy three feet in front of her, then turned and headed down the long shady walkway that led to the Capitol.

———————

"Oh, Daddy, look at the big boat!" Erin, wearing a blue jumper and white ruffled blouse, stood on the upper deck of the ferry, gazing at a huge oil tanker plowing upriver. "Could we go fishing in a boat that big sometime?"

Dylan, noticing his daughter trying to climb for a better view, lifted her and sat her on the top railing, encircling her with both arms. "I don't think so, sugar. That's a ship, and it's not made for fishing. It's made to carry oil, and it goes way out into the Gulf and across the ocean to other countries."

"Dylan, be careful," Susan warned, coming up behind them. "Don't let her fall."

"I won't fall, Mama. Daddy's so strong he could hold me even if I was grown up."

"You tell her, Erin," Dylan said, flexing one bicep through his navy pullover shirt. "I'm so strong, when I go to the beach I kick sand in Charles Atlas's face."

"Who, Daddy?"

"He was a man who had his picture on the back page of comic books a long time ago. He promised that he could change a ninety-eight-pound weakling into a real he-man."

Erin's puzzled frown asked the question for her.

"Never mind," Dylan answered. "It was a long time before you were born."

"Your daddy goes waaay back, sweetheart." Susan grinned. "All the way back to the forties."

Erin giggled at her mother. "Boy, he is old, huh! This is the seventies."

"That's right," Susan agreed, putting her arm around Dylan's waist. "But I think we'll keep him, anyway. Besides, nobody else would take in an old codger like him."

Erin cast her intense blue gaze back toward the tanker. "Where do you think it's going?"

"Probably up to the Esso Refinery in Baton Rouge."

"They make gasoline from the oil, huh?"

"That's right," Dylan replied, wondering how a five-year-old would know that.

As though she knew what he was thinking, Erin explained, "Uncle Emile told me about that. He tells me a lot of stuff when we go get ice cream."

"You keep listening, sugar," Dylan encouraged his daughter. "You'll learn things that'll help you out when you get older."

Erin took her eyes away from the ship, squirming around so she could look at Dylan. "When can we come home, Daddy? I'm tired of New Orleans."

Dylan listened to the deep rumbling of the ferry's diesel engines, churning the muddy Mississippi. He had hoped to avoid it, but deep down he knew Erin would get around to that question. "Pretty soon, sweetheart."

"But I want to go back with you now." A tiny crease formed between Erin's pale eyebrows. "There's no woods or bayous down here. I don't get to play on the dock or go fishing or anything. New Orleans is for grown people, not for kids."

"I think you may be right."

"Then let's go home."

Susan stood next to Dylan, her hand clutching the railing. "Daddy has some work to do, Erin. Just as soon as he's finished, we'll all be together again."

Erin's voice became a small plea. "But I can help you, Daddy. Then you'll get the work done real quick."

Lifting Erin down from the railing, Dylan squatted next to her, gazing directly into her eyes. "You know that you can always trust me, don't you, Erin?"

She nodded, her bottom lip trembling slightly at what she was about to hear.

"Well, this is something I have to do alone." Dylan glanced up at Susan. "And when you're older, I'll explain everything to you. I promise."

Erin nodded her head again, a shadow of sadness flickering in the depths of her eyes. "Okay, Daddy."

"That's my big girl." Dylan picked her up in his arms, pointing across the water. "Look, we're coming into the Canal Street dock. Anybody interested in café au lait and some beignets? Hmmm . . . I can taste them now!"

"Me. I want some!"

"Then we'll go with your mother to some of the antique shops on Royal Street."

"I wanna go to Woolworth's, Daddy."

Dylan turned toward Susan. "Okay with you?"

"Why not? The two of you would just be pestering me to leave before I looked at the first thing."

"Daddy, can I have coffee and milk this time instead of just milk? I'm gonna be in the first grade this year, you know."

"That's right, you sure are. Fine with me, if it's all right with your mother."

Susan nodded. "I bet if you talk to him just right, Erin, your daddy might buy you a new book at Woolworth's."

Erin smiled at her mother. "I already know he will. He always buys me books."

Dylan kissed his daughter on top of her blond head, letting her slide down to the deck. Feeling her tiny warm hand clasping his, he gazed at the approaching city with the wide palm-lined glitter of Canal Street. He listened to the loud swishing of the water past the ferry's bow and offered up a silent prayer that God would protect his family and bring them back home to him soon.

———

Wes Kinchen stood just outside an alcove, leaning against the stone base of North Stadium. From the windows above him he could hear the shouts and laughter of the male students who occupied the dormitory that had earned the nickname "The Rock." A radio inside the nearest window played Frankie Valli's latest hit, "My Eyes Adored You."

Peering into the shadowy darkness, Wes saw a short, furtive figure hurrying toward him next to the stadium wall and as far from the tiger cage across the street as it was possible to get. *Peaches. It's about time.*

The figure stopped, the head pushed forward on its stocky frame. "Mr. Kinchen. Is that you?"

"No, it's the ghost of football seasons past." Wes had paraphrased the line from the Dickens classic off the cuff, but in a sudden burst of insight, he realized that was exactly the figure he represented. He saw himself as an almost derelict, half-crippled linebacker, haunting the night like a ghost from his glory days on the gridiron inside this very stadium. He had lost his wife and son trying to hold on to the fading glory of dreams without substance.

"Mr. Kinchen, are you all right?"

Wes rubbed his face with both hands as if to rid his mind of the sudden thoughts. "I'm just great, Peaches. I was about to give up on you."

Eyes downcast and hands worrying at his car keys, Peaches muttered, "Sorry I'm late. I . . . uh, had some urgent business I had to take care of."

"If you keep dealing that stuff, there's nothing I can do for you when they take you down."

"Aw, c'mon, Mr. Kinchen, you know I don't do that no more," Peaches whined. "Look at me now." He glanced nervously about him as though unseen protean shapes out in the darkness might be stalking him. "I'm here, giving information to a cop. Don't that prove something to you?"

"Yep."

"See, I'm being straight with you, huh?"

"It proves that you want me to keep you from taking a fall

on that possession rap," Wes said in a flat voice. "You know, the one I got you dead-to-rights on."

"Aw, don't talk like that." Peaches sounded as though Wes had just snapped the handcuffs on his scarred wrists. "I got in touch like you told me to, didn't I?"

"That you did, Peaches," Wes agreed, sitting down on the concrete and pulling out a pack of Camels. He stuck one in the corner of his mouth, flicked a kitchen match into flame, and lit it. "Now I'm startin' to wonder why you called this midnight meeting in the first place."

Peaches sat down on the opposite side of the small alcove. "I got something for you." He glanced in the direction of the tiger cage. "You think they got that cage fixed good? I'd hate to see that animal get loose again."

Wes stared through the strands of blue-white smoke rising toward the lofty ceiling of the alcove. "Why don't you just tell me why you set up this meeting, Peaches?"

"I got something to tell you," Peaches said proudly. "Picked it up from one of the junk"—he cleared his throat—"uh, from one of my . . . associates."

"I'm a patient man, Peaches," Wes said, then coughed and stubbed his cigarette out on the floor. "But you are trying me sorely right now."

"California. That's where the dope is goin'."

"What a revelation." Wes shook his head slowly back and forth. "You don't mean to tell me that people out in California use drugs? This is shocking stuff, Peaches."

"Maybe I didn't say it right." Peaches scratched the back of his head with a hooked forefinger. "The people who set up your buddy are gettin' the drugs here and taking them to California to sell them. Make more money that way." He gave Wes a guilty look. "At least that's what they tell me."

"Names, Peaches. I need names."

"I don't have no names."

"What good are you doin' me, then? I already know most

of the drugs coming up from the Gulf are headed for California. New York and Chicago are running close seconds."

"It's somebody new."

"Name. Give me a name."

Peaches shrugged. "Nobody's got a name."

Wes remembered his conversation with Erline. "Somebody in the government, maybe?"

"Could be." Peaches scratched his head again. "But here in Baton Rouge, they's so many people connected to the gover'mint, it don't cut the suspects down much."

"So what have you taught me tonight, Peaches?" Wes rubbed his bad knee with both hands. "Somebody new in the drug business set up my buddy."

"Yeah. That's right."

"Somebody new, with no name and no job that we know of for sure," Wes continued.

"Uh huh."

"I think I'll go ahead and give my report on that possession charge to the district attorney." Wes stared intently at Peaches. "Maybe I can use my time better with somebody else. My investment in you just ain't paying off."

Peaches' lower jaw dropped; his tongue seemed to be made of wood. "I—I . . . uh, uh . . . d-don't do that. I can . . . I mean, we can . . . Please, Mr. Kinchen."

Wes had no intention of filing his report on Peaches, but he knew from years of experience that the only way he could get any useful information from a snitch was to keep the pressure on. "Well," Wes said, rubbing the back of his head, then he stood up, gazing down at Peaches still seated on the concrete floor, "maybe I can give you one more chance."

Peaches got to his feet, a grin crawling across his broad face. "I knew you wouldn't let me down. And I ain't gonna let you down neither, Mr. Kinchen. I'll get out and beat the bushes till I find out something good for you."

Wes stared at the glow of the streetlights out on Stadium Drive. "Uh oh."

Peaches' face dropped, his eyes darting toward the direction Wes was looking. "What's this 'uh oh' business?"

Stepping out of the alcove and glancing in both directions, Wes said, "Looks like somebody left that cage door open again. We'd better—"

Peaches' yowl of terror cut Wes off in midsentence. He watched the little man bolt from the alcove, scurrying along the walkway, short legs churning furiously, his hard heels thudding loudly against the concrete.

12

A NOBLER TIME

"It's like I tried to tell you all along, Dylan." Wes sat on the steps in front of the Memorial Tower, dedicated to the LSU students who died in World War II. "This thing is all about some kind of political vendetta."

Dylan thought about the bullet hole in the windshield of the department's speedboat. He reminded Wes about the night it happened. "I doubt somebody with a political grudge would try to have me assassinated. And I still think the best bet is that somebody out poaching deer just fired a wild shot."

Wes turned troubled eyes on Dylan. "Somebody means to put you in the ground, son. But there's more involved in this than politics, that's for certain." Wes sipped coffee from a Styrofoam cup. "Setting you up on a criminal charge; losing your job with precious little chance of getting another one except maybe pushing a broom somewhere. That should have been enough, if you'd just offended some politician's delicate sensibilities."

Dylan took a bite of a warm doughnut, washing it down with steaming black coffee. "You don't think the shot could have been an accident?"

"About as much as I believe Lee Harvey Oswald's shot was an accident." Wes squinted up at the red sun peeping over the

Corinthian cornices of the law building on the opposite side of the parade ground. "All the evidence says somebody wants you lying on a cold slab, Dylan. We're gonna have to start playing hardball now. Either that or you can buy Susan a nice black dress for your funeral."

Dylan felt a chill in the pit of his stomach. "You know what keeps turning over and over in my mind, Wes?"

Wes sipped his coffee and watched the sunrise.

"What have I done that would make somebody try to take me off the board? In the six years I've been down in Evangeline, nobody's even made a real threat against me."

Placing his cup on the step next to him, Wes yawned and said, "Maybe it's something you didn't . . . or wouldn't do. You ever think about that?"

"I don't know what you're talking about."

"Anybody approach you to let them slide on a pending charge? Or maybe try to get you to look the other way so they could pull some deals in your jurisdiction?"

Dylan thought for a few seconds. "Nothing comes to mind." But something troubled the fuzzy areas of his thoughts like a camera lens that wouldn't quite come into focus.

Wes stood up and stretched. "I've got to get down to New Orleans. Been working a case down there for a couple of months, and I think it's going down today."

"I was wondering why you wanted to meet so early. You never were one for watching the sunrise."

"See if you can come up with anything while I'm gone. I'll be back as soon as I can." Wes picked up the cup, crumpled it, and tossed it into a trash can housed in concrete. "How's Emile handling this?"

Dylan pictured the concern on his old friend's face. "Doing the best he can."

"He's a good man," Wes said, glancing at the clock on the tower behind him. "But he's been handling things in Evangeline for so long, I expect it's hard for him to realize how much the world's changed outside that sleepy little town."

"He knows," Dylan said, touching his forehead with the tips of his fingers, "but I don't think it ever really registers in his heart that people can do the things they do to each other, even after all his years in law enforcement."

"Good for him," Wes said. "Sometimes I wish I hadn't seen what I have"—his eyes seemed to mirror dark thoughts and old sorrows—"but it's too late to change that now."

———————

Dylan sat in his Volkswagen, parked on Spanish Town Road behind a screen of azaleas. In bright daylight, he had watched Becky climb the stairs and go into her apartment in the Pentagon. Now the sun had slipped down behind the cane fields across the river, and the April night was pleasantly cool. Across the formal gardens to the north, the dome lights of the Capitol building glimmered against a black sky four hundred feet above the city.

During the long wait, Dylan found he was talking to himself. "I hope you're not a part of this, Becky. We've been friends too long. Don't let me down.

"Wouldn't your daddy be proud of you now, Dylan." He pictured his white-haired father working in a cold December rain, unloading ships on the Robin Street Wharf in New Orleans. "You've lost your job, had to send your wife and daughter away because somebody's out to settle an old score with you, and now you're tailing your best friend from high school on the wild assumption that she's behind all your troubles."

Dylan thought of the walking drudgery his days would be without Susan and Erin. "Well, you won't have long to worry about that if they send you to prison. Soon as word gets out that you're an ex-cop, somebody'll slip a blade between your ribs.

"If you get caught talking to yourself, you'll be spending the days from now till your trial in the nut ward. Keep your thoughts to yourself." Dylan rubbed his face with both hands, yawned, and poured coffee from a red thermos bottle into a plastic cup. Then he turned on the radio and listened to Carole King sing her first big hit, "It's Too Late," as he stared through the windshield at the Pentagon. Constructed in 1819 by General Zachary Taylor, it reminded him of a simpler and perhaps nobler time.

Finally, in the glow of the streetlamps, Dylan watched Becky hurry down the stairs, climb into her rented sedan, and head south on River Road. Dylan followed her at a safe distance, hoping she wouldn't drive fast enough to leave the little four-cylinder Volkswagen behind.

Passing by the turnoff that led over the levee to the old ferry landing, no longer in use since the new I–10 bridge had been completed, Dylan followed Becky across the new bridge, then south on Highway 1, driving toward Evangeline. When they reached the town, Becky headed west toward the Basin. Dylan kept his distance in the open country outside of town, then watched the headlights of her car swing south again, following the intracoastal waterway.

When Dylan reached the intersection, he turned north toward home. Passing through the cane fields, flat and barren now after the autumn harvest, he pushed the little car up to seventy. To his left, a sliver of moon hung over the Basin. Clouds, their edges silvered by pale light, swept across the sky from the south.

Pulling into his shed, Dylan cut the engine, grabbed the twelve-gauge pump shotgun from the backseat, dumped a few shells into the pocket of his Marine fatigue jacket, and ran out to the dock. He leaped down into the aluminum bateau, started the ten-horse Mercury on the third pull, and headed down the bayou.

Out in the open water, Dylan could see by the pale light of moon and stars, but when he reached the narrow bayou that led to the Cajun village under a canopy of tree limbs, he strapped a hunter's headlight on and followed its thin white beam through the thick darkness of the channel.

Ten minutes later, he heard the drone of a powerful engine turning from the main waterway into the narrow bayou. Knowing they'd never hear his small engine over the roar of their own, Dylan gunned the Mercury to top speed. He glanced back occasionally, the roar of their big engine getting progressively louder with each slow bend of the bayou.

Fifty yards before reaching the village, Dylan flicked the headlight off, backed into the mouth of a small outlet screened by overhanging willow limbs, cut his engine, and waited. In less than a minute the big boat roared past, its bright light illuminating the bayou from bank to bank. Its wake suddenly thrust the bateau upward, banging Dylan's head against an overhanging limb. He grabbed the limb with one hand, holding on to the boat with the other, steadying it until the rocking subsided.

Dylan felt a warm trickle of blood down the side of his face. "What a great start!" he whispered to himself. "They busted my head open and don't even know I'm here. What'll they do if they actually find me?

"Here I am out in the middle of the Basin, talking to myself again." Dylan stood up in the boat, tying it to the limb that had just banged the side of his head. He slung the shotgun over his shoulder, felt the reassuring weight of the Colt automatic on his belt, and stepped out into the night woods.

Using the bayou as a guide, Dylan crept toward the village, following the edge of the clearing around to the office building near the dock. Peering through the screen of leaves and underbrush, in the faint light of sixty-watt bulbs he saw Becky and two men standing near the big speedboat. He could hear the murmur of their conversation but could make out no words.

Then the three of them walked to the end of the dock and on toward the office located forty feet from the edge of the woods where he lay hidden. After they had stepped inside, someone flicked a switch and the windows glowed with yellow light. Dylan leaned the shotgun against a tree, then crawled slowly across the open ground to the back of the building. Through the slightly open window he could hear the sound of voices.

" . . . into Lake Palourde and on through Lake Verret, then we tie into the Intracoastal." The man's voice held all the warmth of a hangman's noose. The accent was Latin American. "Or we can go directly up the Atchafalaya. There's a hundred ways to head east or west if we do that."

"And there's a thousand places to hide if someone picks up your trail."

Rayburn, Dylan thought. *Why would somebody with his kind of money risk everything to get involved in something that could put him away for life?*

"Picks up our trail?" The accent was heavy on sarcasm. "You been watching too many westerns, Rayburn. Next thing, you'll be calling me 'buckaroo.' "

Rayburn's oiled voice held an undertone of embarrassment. "I find that insults are counterproductive to any business enterprise. Why don't we try to keep things on a professional level."

Laughter spilled out of the other speaker. "You a real comedian. Keep things on a pro-fesh-ee-nal level," the voice mocked. "You would maybe like to see my pro-fesh-ee-nal license for this line of work?"

" 'Hey, good lookin', wha'cha got cookin'?' "

At the sound of the voice coming from the edge of the woods on the far side of the clearing, Dylan dropped to his belly and flattened out in the shadow of the building. Keeping his head down, he peered through the smoky light, listening to the sound of singing out in the dark.

A tall, broad-shouldered man wearing a cowboy hat and a heavy revolver strapped to his waist ambled slowly out of the woods and headed for the office. A Ruger .44 magnum carbine hung over his shoulder on a leather strap. Dylan held his breath as the man crossed out of his sight on the opposite side of the office.

"Travis, you're being paid to keep an eye on this place," Rayburn snarled from inside the office. "We've been here for fifteen minutes. Where were you?"

The man's voice rumbled in his chest. "Uh, I had to use the, uh . . . facilities."

"Well, next time . . ."

Dylan didn't wait for Rayburn to complete his verbal discipline of the man but stood up and ran lightly on the balls of his feet over to the woods. Stepping inside the screen of tree limbs and underbrush, he grabbed the shotgun and lay down next to the trunk of a towering beech tree.

"You hear something out there?" The rumbling voice cut Rayburn's speech off.

Dylan watched from his hiding place as the big man walked around the corner of the office, unslinging his rifle. He snatched a flashlight from his back pocket, letting its bright beam follow the edge of the clearing.

When the light reached him, Dylan pressed his face flat against the ground, then looked up as it passed on by. Rayburn had joined the big man.

"I thought you heard something out here."

The man took a few steps directly toward Dylan, the beam cutting a swath of brightness out into the dark woods. Then he flicked it off and jammed it into his back pocket. "Guess I was wrong."

Dylan watched the two men return to the office. Five minutes later, the big man stepped out with a folding chair, placed it facing the office door, and sat down. From this position he could watch the woods where Dylan lay hidden as well as the dock where three boats were moored.

Dylan waited thirty minutes. Finally, he decided that the

man had been given orders not to move until the three inside had finished their business. He got up from the ground and made his way quietly back to the bateau. An hour later, the big speedboat roared past his hiding place, its spotlight sweeping through the night.

"Still think your old girlfriend's Snow White, Dylan?" Wes sat on his single bed rubbing his .357 with a soft cloth. A can of Three-In-One oil and a cleaning kit lay on a section of folded newspaper next to him.

"No," Dylan said softly. He sat at the tiny dinette near the sink, stove, and refrigerator that were built into the wall.

Wes held his pistol up to the light, inspecting the barrel for cleanliness. Running an oiled cloth through it one more time, he began carefully inserting six hollow points into the cylinder. "You know what your problem is, son?"

"Which one?" Dylan mumbled, his expression as blank as the walls of Wes's apartment.

Wes laughed, clicked the cylinder of his pistol into place, and said, "You got too much faith in people, especially your old school friends."

Dylan stared at Wes, wondering where he had gone wrong in the areas of friendship and loyalty. "I was brought up to believe that was a good thing, Wes."

Shoving his pistol into its holster, Wes grinned at Dylan. "You're thinking about the fifties, son. This is the Me Decade, the Self-Serving Seventies."

"You're telling me friendship doesn't matter anymore?" Dylan pulled his .45 out of its holster, ejected the clip, slid the receiver back, and tossed the automatic onto the bed next to Wes. "Give this a quick going-over, will you?"

"Sure, friendships matter, but for most of the people I run across, not as much as the big Me."

"Let's face it, Wes. In your, or *our*, line of work, we're not likely to meet the typical American."

"True." Wes broke the Colt down and began cleaning the parts. "But we've never had this self-enlightenment stuff before in this country."

"I guess up till now people were too busy making a living to worry about things like that."

"That's part of it," Wes agreed, squeezing a couple of drops of oil down the weapon's barrel. He gave Dylan a crooked grin. "There's an ex-used car salesman named John Paul Rosenberg from Philadelphia, changed his name to Werner Erhard, and started those EST seminars. Ever heard of him?"

Dylan nodded. "Vaguely."

"He's pretty typical of the times, I think. He concentrates strictly on me, me, me. His seminars are supposed to help you 'get rid of old baggage.'" The smile was on Wes's face again. "I think the 'old baggage' just happens to be things like loyalty, integrity, and telling the truth."

Dylan thought of Richard Nixon's resignation just two years before. "Who'd have thought the President would ever lie to the people or use the kind of language he did in the White House? I guess Americans still think the President should be above that sort of thing."

"Well, at least he had the decency to resign."

"I felt kind of sorry for him . . . and his family." Dylan saw again the pained smile on the President's face. "I know the press has an obligation to let the people know the truth, but where do you draw the line? Kennedy's indiscretions never made the newspapers when he was in office, and they never exposed Roosevelt's either, or his disability. These things weren't in the same category as Watergate, but I think it's just as much a loss of respect for the Presidency as anything else."

"I think it's just a loss of respect," Wes muttered, locking the pistol's receiver into place, "for everything."

Dylan's mind suddenly jumped to the night's work ahead

of them. "You're pretty sure these people are going to make a run tonight, Wes?"

"Well," Wes began, taking a rumpled sheet of paper from the pocket of his khaki shirt, "according to your girlfriend's work schedule that she made for you and—"

"Wes," Dylan cut in on him, "let's leave out all the little terms of endearment, all right?"

"You're right, sorry. Anyhow, using this schedule, we know there wouldn't be any runs when you were supposed to be checking on the village."

"But I don't work there anymore. That schedule is meaningless now."

"Any change they make could cause problems on down the line," Wes explained. "It might affect a dozen or more people. That's why I think they'll stick to it. Besides, Peaches thinks they're making a run tonight."

"All right," Dylan said as Wes tossed him the Colt. He checked the clip and shoved it into the pistol's butt. "You still think we shouldn't get backup."

"That's *exactly* what I think. If this guy's connections are good enough, he'll find out we're on to their little enterprise before we ever make it to the Basin."

"I guess you're right. Just the two of us, though. Think we can handle them?"

Wes reached underneath his bed and hauled out a heavy canvas duffel bag. Opening it, he grabbed an M–16 and a short-barreled automatic weapon with a long clip. "This oughta be enough firepower to take on whatever they've got."

"What's that little automatic?"

Wes hefted the weapon. "Uzi. The IDF uses these. Right up there with the AK–47 for dependability . . . maybe better. Just a little easier to handle."

"IDF. That's the Israel Defense Force, right?" Dylan answered his own question. "Where'd you get a gun like that? Only place I've ever seen one is on television."

"Good connections." Wes tossed the M–16 to Dylan. "You wanna use this?"

Dylan checked the safety, ejected the clip, and pulled the receiver back. "I'd better. Emile let me keep one that belongs to the department, but it'd probably be best not to have it along in case things get . . . official."

"Right." Wes stood up, grabbing a long black coat from a nail driven into the wall. "Well, that's about enough of this chitchat. Let's hit 'em, son."

"We'd better take out 'Buffalo Bob' before the heavy hitters show up." Wes, standing in the edge of the woods next to Dylan, pointed with his Uzi toward the little office building the man called Travis had just entered after making his rounds. "When I get into position, you make some noise."

Wes ran hunched over to the front of the office and took up a position at the side of the door. Moving along the woods until he was closer to the front door, Dylan found a chunk of fallen limb and hurled it in an end-over-end arc. The limb banged against the wall just below the roofline.

Travis came lumbering out the door, holding the Ruger carbine at port arms, stumbled over Wes's outstretched leg, and sprawled face down on the raw, bulldozed dirt. Wes leaped on the big man's back, thumped him on the head with the stock of his Uzi, then snatched the heavy revolver from the man's belt.

Dylan had left the woods in a dead run before Travis hit the ground and now stood next to him holding the rifle. "He still breathing?"

"I just gave him a little love tap," Wes answered, pulling a roll of duct tape from his pocket. He wound the tape around the man's hands behind his back, ripped it from the roll, and taped the end in place. "Give me a hand here. We've gotta get him out of sight before the rest show up."

Dylan helped Wes drag the big man twenty yards into the woods, placing him in a sitting position against a tree trunk on the side opposite the village. Wes taped his ankles together, then wound two strips of tape around his waist and chest, securing him to the tree. Then he taped his mouth tightly closed. "That oughta keep him quiet for a while."

"You sure he's all right?" Dylan watched Travis's shallow breathing, his head lolling loosely to one side.

Taking a red bandanna from the back pocket of his Levi's, Wes blindfolded the man. "No sense in his being able to identify us"—he glanced at Dylan—"in case things go bad." He slapped the man's cheeks several times.

Travis groaned, lifted his head slowly, then twisted violently against his bonds. His muffled attempts at speech proved no more successful than his struggles to free himself.

Wes spoke in a flat, dead voice. "Don't fight it, partner. You'll be all right. We'll send somebody for you later." He leaned closer. "You understand me?"

Travis nodded.

"Good. You just sit tight now and you'll be fine." Wes stood up. "And if you hear a little gunfire, don't let it bother you. This tree'll stop any stray bullets coming this way."

Wes motioned to Dylan with his head, and they walked through the short span of woods to the village. "I've got this feeling they'll come tonight. And when they do, we've got two advantages—the element of surprise and having the time to take up defensive positions where we can enfilade the area around the dock."

The military jargon describing tactical combat took Dylan back to his boot camp days. He could almost hear the grizzled old Marine sergeant instructing them in the most efficient ways of killing other human beings. He glanced about the village. "What about the general store and the church?"

Wes took a quick inventory of the buildings nearest the dock. "You've still got some of that ol' military eye left, son.

We can catch 'em in a crossfire if they try to rush the village."

"Your choice," Dylan said, pointing to the wooden structures with the muzzle of his rifle.

"You take the church." Wes checked his extra clips and headed toward the general store, then turned around. "I'd like to take them without firing a shot, Dylan." His lips were a thin, pale line. "But I wouldn't count on it."

Dylan walked down to the bayou's edge, squatted, and scooped a handful of dark "gumbo mud." Then he smeared it on his face, neck, and the tops of his hands to cut down on reflected light in those exposed areas of his body.

"Good idea," Wes said, following suit before he took up his position in the store.

Walking over to the little church with its white steeple and stained-glass windows, Dylan gazed at the fake village bathed in hazy light. He entered the darkened church and dragged a pew over to one of the open front windows. Positioning the back of the pew toward the window for extra protection, he sat down and stared at the lights wavering on the bayou that would bring night-loving, violent people to him.

13

THE GRAVE

The boats came a few minutes past midnight. Dylan heard the whine of their engines far out in the Basin. Then the distant whine became a muted roar, and the roar found a home in the sleek black hulls of two identical speedboats, trailing wakes white as ginned cotton against the dark surface of the bayou.

Throttling back their engines, the drivers idled their boats lazily toward the old tires hanging along the edge of the dock. As they bumped the tires, men in dark clothing with automatic weapons slung over their shoulders leaped onto the dock and tied off at bow and stern.

Four other men joined the two men on the docks, two of them armed as the first two. Dylan stared at the taller of the two men without weapons. He was lean, well dressed, and seemed to hold himself aloof from the other five men. A fedora, worn low on his forehead, cast his face into shadow, but Dylan recognized his gait as he walked along next to his shorter companion behind the four armed men.

Alert now for Wes's signal, Dylan flicked the M–16's safety down to full automatic. Just as the first four men walked down the dock steps onto the bank, Wes bellowed from his position in the general store, "State Police! Drop your weapons!"

Almost immediately the first four men raked the general

store with automatic fire. Dylan saw the white bursts of Wes's return fire and then a sudden calmness fell on him. All the training and all the experience he had gained in firefights in Vietnam took over. He saw the four men leaping behind pilings at the edge of the dock, and he enfiladed the area, using short bursts.

A scream rose above the sound of heavy firing as one of the men threw his arms upward, flung backward into the water by the impact of the M–16 rounds. Dylan slammed a fresh clip home and fired two more short bursts, but the other three men had vanished beneath the flooring of the dock.

Dylan watched the two unarmed men run the final twenty feet to the boats and leap down into the one moored farthest from the shoreline. One of the men beneath the dock waded out and grabbed his fallen comrade. Dylan lined his sights up on the man's chest but couldn't fire as the man pulled his wounded or dead friend back beneath the dock.

Wes shouted, "You all right?"

Dylan answered with a burst of fire at a man running from beneath the dock toward a stack of lumber near the water's edge. Wes cut loose with his Uzi, tearing out chunks of dirt and churning the water just behind the running man. But he made it to safety unharmed and immediately began laying down covering fire on the church and the store as his two friends dragged the man Dylan had shot back toward the waiting boats.

Dylan watched the men dump their friend over the side into the first boat, then move around to the stern so they could clamber into the boat out of the line of fire. The man behind the stack of lumber continued his sporadic bursts until both engines started, the boats backed out into the channel, and they roared away down the bayou.

Above the sound of the engines, Dylan heard the man behind the stack of lumber screaming in Spanish. Then he stopped, and there remained only the fading whine of the engines, and finally silence.

Five minutes later, Dylan heard a board squeak behind him. Whirling around, he could almost hear the M-16 barking and feel it thumping against his shoulder as he began to squeeze the trigger, then he jerked his finger away. "Wes! Are you crazy? I almost killed you!"

Wes grinned and stuck a Camel between his lips. "Whadda you think we should do about Pancho out there?"

Dylan glanced out at the lumber. No sight or sound came from the man abandoned by his friends. "You stay here and keep him pinned down. I'll go out the back and get into the woods. When I get to the edge of the bayou, I should have him in my sights."

"What then?"

Thinking of the danger Susan and Erin were in with men like this free to ply their lethal trade, Dylan said, "He'll give up his weapon . . . or I'll shoot him."

Wes lit his cigarette, staring at Dylan through the smoke. "I believe you, son."

Dylan turned and went out the back door of the church, then, using the buildings and stacks of construction materials as shields, made his way to the woods. Once inside the cover of the trees and underbrush, he walked quickly to the water's edge, standing just inside the woods. Peering out through the leafy screen, he saw his enemy crouched behind the stack of lumber.

Dylan flicked the safety of the M–16 to automatic and fountained the water behind the man with a short burst. The man spun on his heels, pointing his weapon toward his unseen attacker in the woods, his face frozen in fear and disbelief.

Hearing Wes shouting in Spanish, Dylan assumed he was demanding the man's surrender. The man turned toward the sound of Wes's voice, then quickly stood up and fired his weapon at the church.

Lost in the heat of combat now, Dylan emptied his clip into the stack of lumber, sending bullets whining like mad hornets over the man's head. Chips and splinters of wood showered the man, who screamed in terror, dropped his weapon, and stood up, hands clasped behind his head.

Dylan slapped a full clip home, snicked a round into the chamber, and walked out of the woods, the muzzle of his rifle held steady on the man's chest. Wes had run from the church and now stood behind the man at the opposite end of the stack of lumber.

Ten minutes later, the prisoner lay bound and gagged on the damp ground in front of the church. Dylan and Wes sat inside on the pew that Dylan had used as his firing position.

Wes glanced out the window at the bound man lying still and seemingly content in front of the church. "He's thinking that his boss's lawyer will have him turned loose in a few days."

"How do you know what he's thinking?"

"I've seen the process too many times not to know." Wes drew on his cigarette, its tip glowing red in the near dark. "He won't have a record of any kind. Once they're busted in this country, they replace them with somebody else. It'll be a high bond, but he'll make it, and we'll never see him again."

Dylan gazed out at the man who looked as comfortable and as placid as if he were on vacation relaxing on a beach. "What's the alternative?"

"We make him talk."

"From what I know about these guys, that might not be so easy."

"The money, the women, the big cars," Wes spoke in a flat voice, his eyes cold and remote, "they come and go. But life—" he glanced at his prisoner—"that's the one constant they hold to . . . the only thing that really matters to them."

"We can't kill him, Wes."

"You're right, *we* can't." Wes's mouth drew back in a thin, bitter smile.

Dylan felt a chill at the back of his neck. "I couldn't let you do that . . . commit murder."

"You think he wouldn't kill us in a second if he had the chance?" Wes glanced at the man again. "And he'd do it in ways that most humans couldn't even dream of."

"We aren't going to kill this man, Wes." Dylan spoke with a finality that registered in Wes's expression.

Acting as though he hadn't heard Dylan's words, Wes said, "Let's take him someplace and get started."

"What's wrong with here?"

Wes bared his teeth in what passed for a grin. "It's always more effective when you blindfold them and take them for a ride somewhere. They understand that. It's the way they take care of business themselves."

"So, where we goin'?"

Wes shrugged. "You got any ideas?"

Dylan thought a few seconds, nodded slowly, and followed Wes outside.

An hour and twenty minutes later, Dylan backed Wes's pickup out of the shed next to his house, then drove toward Evangeline. "You sure he can't get loose back there?"

Wes glanced through the back glass at their prisoner, lying beneath a heavy tarp in the bed of the pickup. "Naw. He's flat on his back for this trip, but just in case, I took a couple of loops around his neck and tied him to the spare tire rack."

"That oughta do it."

"Where you takin' us?"

"Someplace pretty. You'll like it."

"Pretty I can do without," Wes said, glancing again at their prisoner. "Private is what I'm looking for."

"This is about as private as you can get."

"That's all we need, son." Wes looked as though he had just discovered some marvelous secret. "This is gonna be more fun than bustin' bones on an Ole Miss quarterback."

Dylan turned left on the road to Evangeline. "Let's just get the information we need and put this man in jail. I don't want to make a party out of it."

"What's the matter with you?" Wes's face held an expression of mild disbelief. "You know what an opportunity we have here? You know how rare it is to take one of these guys alive? Usually they're the ones holding all the cards."

Dylan knew he was fighting for a losing cause in keeping the conversation with Wes alive.

"We can send a message to that whole bunch that think this country is just another one of their little playgrounds." He jerked his thumb back at the prisoner. "Tough for him, he's the one that got caught."

Although Dylan wanted more than anything to secure the safety of his wife and daughter, he knew he couldn't let Wes take this man's life.

———————

Dylan turned into the gravel drive leading back to the river. On his left, Mattie's little cabin stood dark and quiet, bathed in the faint light of the westering moon. Gravel crunched beneath the tires of the truck as he drove through the dark tunnel of trees. In the glare of the headlights, a bobcat flashed across the road, disappearing into the thick underbrush.

"First time I ever saw one of those outside a zoo," Wes observed.

"They're pretty skittish all right," Dylan said, thinking of what an efficient predator the big cat was.

"So this is the ol' homestead." Wes gazed through the windshield, seemingly fascinated by the ride leading through thick woods.

"This is a private road," Dylan told him, "and it leads all the way back to the river."

"It's just what we're looking for, all right." Wes seemed as cheerful as if they were going on a picnic. "You think I could bring Chet camping up here sometime?"

"Sure. Anytime you want." As they passed his grandparents' cottage, Dylan felt a pang of guilt, wondering how they would have felt about the terrified stranger who was bound and gagged in the back of the truck. The pickup rumbled over an old railroad trestle, floored by his grandfather, that crossed a creek.

Wes gazed down at the water. "Hey, who built this bridge?"

"This road used to be a railroad. When it went out of business, the company took the rails and crossties, but the property reverted back to my grandfather."

A quarter mile past the trestle, Dylan turned south, driving along a rutted and abandoned logging road for a hundred yards beneath towering pines and oaks, then parked in a clearing on the bank of the river.

"This is just perfect." Wes's expression was that of a ten-year-old boy with a new bicycle.

Dylan got out of the truck and walked over to the edge of the bluff. Thirty feet below, the river gurgled over a fallen log. The waning moon cast a shimmering path across the water's surface. Hearing a grunting noise, he turned back to see Wes carrying the little man over his shoulder and dumping him on the ground in the glare of the headlights. Then he tossed a shovel on the ground next to him.

"What's this all about, Wes?"

"You'll find out soon enough," Wes said, kneeling next to his prisoner.

Before Dylan had time to react, Wes pulled his revolver from its holster, pulled the hammer back, and pressed the muzzle against the man's forehead.

"Wes, stop, you can't—"

In the quiet of the glade, the explosion of the .357 magnum shell jarred Dylan. Stunned by Wes's unexpected action, Dylan stared at the man on the ground. The side of his forehead was blackened by the muzzle blast where Wes had turned the barrel

183

aside just before firing the pistol. He writhed in the dead leaves and pine needles, a muffled keening escaping his taped mouth.

"Are you crazy?" Dylan shouted.

Wes gave him a sly grin. "Just wanted to get his attention, you know . . . before we get down to business." He leaned down and ripped the tape from the man's eyes.

The man stared up at Wes with a look of terror and hope-lessness.

"We can't do this, Wes."

Wes growled something at the man in Spanish, then mo-tioned for Dylan to follow him around to the other side of the truck. "This man would murder your little girl and eat a bur-rito while he was doing it. You can't show him any sign of weakness, son. If you do, you're gonna ruin the whole show here, and we won't get a peep out of him."

"I can't be a party to torture, Wes." Dylan held his steely gaze. "What do you have in mind?"

"I'm gonna start by having him dig his own grave. That oughta bring him around."

"What if it doesn't?"

"I haven't thought that far ahead yet." Wes glanced back in the direction of the man on the ground. "You just keep in mind what this little worm would do to your family if his boss told him to."

"Where'd you learn Spanish?"

Wes grinned sanely this time. "The little señorita in the language department at LSU." He headed back around the truck. "Knowledge is a wonderful thing, son."

As Dylan walked past the man, he stared up at him with pleading eyes. Dylan glanced over at Wes and shrugged as though things were beyond his control now. Sitting down at the base of a pine, he watched Wes tie a rope around the man's neck, securing the other end to the bumper of the pickup, then free his arms and legs and hand him a shovel.

Wes pointed at the ground and spoke to the man in Spanish. "Dig!"

The man was petrified, trying to mumble something through his taped mouth.

Shaking his head, Wes told the man, "I know a tough guy like you won't talk—won't tell us a thing, so just dig." He glanced around the little clearing. "You gotta admit, though, it's a beautiful place to be buried."

Two hours later, the man lay in the bottom of a freshly dug hole, covered with dirt up to his chin, his straining eyes filled with a terrible light.

Wes finally jumped down into the hole and ripped the tape from his mouth. "You wanna tell me who you're working for, partner?"

Words spilled from the man's mouth. He told his story in broken English, answering every question Wes asked him in detail. When he had finished, Wes pulled him out of the pit, gave him a pen and pad, and instructed him to write an abbreviated version. When the man had finished, he retaped his hands and feet, dumping him back into the pickup's bed beneath the tarp.

Wes spoke in a soft voice. "Man, do I feel silly. Who'd have thought he knew English?"

"You think any of this will stick?"

Wes glanced at the truck. "I think he doesn't know enough about the law not to give the same story to the DEA or whoever finally gets ahold of him." He slapped Dylan on the shoulder. "What matters is we've got what we need to shut this bunch down and save your hide to boot."

On the way out, Dylan drove onto the old trestle, the tires rumbling across the rough plank flooring.

"Stop a minute, will you?" Wes opened his door and started to slide out of the cab.

Dylan jammed the brakes. "What're you doing?"

Without answering, Wes reached over into the bed of the

pickup, lifted the little man out, and, grasping him by both ankles, dangled him over the edge of the trestle. Squeaking with fear, the man answered three or four rapid-fire questions from Wes.

"All right, partner," Wes said, hefting the man back into the pickup and covering him with the canvas, "you can take it easy from now on."

When Wes had climbed back into the cab, Dylan asked, "What was that all about?"

The faint glow of the dashboard lights shadowed the hard, craggy planes of Wes's face. "Just wanted to make sure I got the same answers to the questions I'd already asked him."

Dylan drove on, passing the cottage where he had spent those long, indolent summers so long ago. "Well, what's the verdict on our boy in the back?"

Wes glanced over his shoulder at the canvas-covered lump that had become his newest informant. "I believe we've made an honest man out of him."

———

Dylan stood on the roadside leaning on his shovel and watching the red glow of the taillights on Wes's pickup growing smaller and smaller. They finally winked out in the distance. Feeling a great weariness suddenly press down on him almost like a solid weight, he turned and walked toward the shed to put the shovel away.

Stepping inside the tin-roofed building, Dylan sat down on an upturned galvanized bucket just inside the door and leaned back against the wall. He smelled the damp earth and the musty scent of the old timbers. A breeze blew in through the door that opened toward the bayou.

Along with the weariness, Dylan felt an oppressive sense of guilt. He called back the image of the petrified little man, covered up to his chin in raw dirt, down in the grave he had been forced to dig for himself. Dylan saw again the heart-stopping terror deep inside his dark eyes. But he would do it again to ensure the safety of Susan and Erin and to have them home again.

Standing up, Dylan found himself still holding on to the shovel. Just as he started to hang it on the wall between two nails, he caught a faint glint of light on metal near the door that opened onto the path leading to the cabin. *Knife blade.* The thought leaped into the forefront of his mind. A shadow ripped itself loose from the dark wall, leaping toward him.

Dylan grabbed the shovel handle with both hands, parrying the slashing blow of the knife. He heard the heavy blade thud into the handle inches from his chest. Stepping aside, he used the shovel as he had the cudgel sticks in boot camp, thumping the man across his left shoulder with the flat of the blade.

The man with the knife stumbled but didn't go down. Spinning around, he made another lunge at Dylan with the knife, this time thrusting forward as a swordsman would. Dylan gave the man's wrist a glancing blow with the shovel handle, breaking his grip on the knife, but the big man's momentum carried him into Dylan, sending him crashing against the wall.

Dylan's head bounced off a two-by-four stud. As he hit the ground, holding the shovel in a defensive position, he caught a glimpse of his dark adversary darting through the doorway that led to the road.

Scrambling to his feet, Dylan dropped the shovel, snatched his .45 from its holster, and ran through the door. Outside, he saw nothing but the long dark ribbon of road in either direction, the woods on the other side, and the long grass bending in the night wind.

"They just don't assassinate cops." Emile hung up the phone and sipped his second cup of coffee. "Not as a general rule, they don't. Could be a whole new breed of criminal mind out there, though. These South and Central Americans don't seem to play by the same rules as our homegrown drug dealers. By the way, that call was from the lab. No prints on the knife."

"I expected that." Dylan shrugged. "The Feds put our boy into their witness protection program yesterday as soon as they had questioned him enough to verify that he was for real," he explained, staring out the window of Emile's office at the early morning light glinting across the storefronts of Evangeline. "Why wait until now to try to take me out, though? Why not when I was out patrolling in the Basin?"

"You've forgotten that hole in the boat's windshield?"

Dylan shook his head. "No, but for some reason I just don't think it's got anything to do with the drug runners."

"You think your friend with the knife last night was one of their hit men?"

"Maybe, I don't know." Dylan shrugged. "I know their decisions are basically business decisions, so how does it turn a profit for them to do away with an insignificant deputy in an out-of-the-way parish? I never even came close to taking one of them down until Wes stepped into the picture."

Emile rubbed his chin between thumb and forefinger. "Maybe you're right. Or maybe somebody had a contract out on you and didn't get the word that your and Wes's boy had given them up already."

Dylan walked over and sat down in the chair next to Emile's desk. "Wes called first thing this morning. The Feds intercepted eleven shipments and made twenty-seven arrests last night along the Florida, Louisiana, and Texas coasts and on the intracoastal waterways."

Nodding, a grim smile on his face, Emile said, "They moved fast all right. Nailed them before they could get word out that one of their own had turned on them. Didn't have time to change their schedules." He gave Dylan a somber look. "Let's give it another day or two. They'll know by then that it's all out of your hands. You should be all right after that."

"I've got to see Becky," Dylan said, taking comfort in the

thought that his ordeal was almost over. "I think I can get enough information out of her to nail the only local man our informant couldn't identify."

"Just don't go home for a couple of nights."

"I'll stay with Wes." Dylan grinned. "I don't think they'll come within a mile of his place, even if they find out I'm there."

14

SEASON OF LIGHT

Dylan climbed the stairs to the second story gallery of the Pentagon. Knocking on Becky's door, he gazed out at a tugboat churning upriver behind a string of barges. He listened to the traffic behind him on North Third, then heard the muted sound of high heels clicking on hardwood inside the apartment.

Becky opened the door, a silver-screen smile posing on her face. "Why, Dylan, whatever are you doing here?"

Dylan's gaze was at once cold and remote, yet as intensely personal as an unspeakable secret. "No more screenplays, Becky. This is the real thing."

Becky struggled to hold on to the smile, but it wilted and slipped from her face under Dylan's dry gaze. Then she tried on her injured-and-becoming-indignant role. "I'm just a little bit tired of you believing every wild tale you hear—"

Dylan cut her off with an abbreviated list of names the informer had given them as well as the dates, times, and methods of the most recent drug shipments.

Stunned, all of her calculated confidence deserting her, Becky placed her hand to her throat and backed slowly away from Dylan into the apartment. She collapsed on the sofa, holding her face in her hands. In a few seconds she began

191

trembling, then rocking back and forth, weeping softly.

Dylan went to the kitchen, filled a glass from the tap, and brought it to her. "Here, Becky, drink this."

Becky turned her tearstained face toward Dylan, her eyes already puffy and slightly glazed from the impact of what he had just told her. She took the glass, holding it in her hands, seemingly too numb to know what to do with it. Glancing at Dylan, she began to cry again.

Dylan pulled a wingback chair over in front of the couch and sat down facing Becky. He put enough distance between them so he could not reach over and comfort her. In a few minutes, he asked, "Why did you do it, Becky?"

Becky took a deep breath, shuddering as she released it. "It's so . . . so complicated."

"You'd pick the drugs up at the village, take them to California on one of your business trips, and deliver them to the West Coast dealer. Is that about it?"

"I—I thought Ralph loved me," Becky blurted out. "He said he was going to leave his wife."

Surprised by what he had just heard, Dylan surmised that he knew far less than Becky thought he did. He decided to keep quiet and see where she would take them.

"I was so afraid of my husband after two years of living with his rages. And I couldn't seem to get him out of my life, no matter what I did." Becky took a swallow of the water. "And we were so far in debt, there was no way I could pay off the bills with what I made at the studio."

Becky drank from her glass, her eyes unfocused, giving her the appearance of a blind person. "When I first met Ralph it . . . it was like I'd finally found some kind of hope. He treated me like I was someone so special to him. And"—a tear slipped down her cheek as she continued—"I felt so safe when I was with him. He told me he was going to leave his wife so we could be together all the time. All that southern charm . . . I'd been away so long and been married so . . . I'd forgotten what it was to be treated like a lady." She turned her gaze slowly on Dylan. "Is that too much to ask, Dylan? Just to be treated like a lady?"

"No." Dylan knew she was in too deep. He hated to think of what lay ahead for her. "No, it's not too much to ask, Becky."

She gazed again out the window, longingly, as though she wanted very badly to be on one of the ships plowing downriver toward New Orleans and beyond to the open sea. "Anyway, not long after we started working together on the village, he told me about a way he knew that I could get out of debt . . . and make some real money for myself"—she glanced at Dylan—"for both of us.

"I never meant to get you involved, Dylan." She grasped for his hand, but it was just out of reach. She sat back on the couch, clasping her hands together in her lap. "Then you came along that night and saved my life . . . and, well, everything just seemed to happen without my planning any of it."

She looked at Dylan again, her eyes filling with tears. "All those come-ons—all the phony flirtations. I'm so sorry I did that, Dylan."

Unable to hold his gaze, she stared at her hands. "Ralph told me to do that. Try to get you to go along with us." This time she met his eyes. "But I knew you'd never do anything like that, no matter how I tried to persuade you." She stood up quickly and walked over to the window. "That's when Ralph came up with the idea to set you up in my apartment."

Dylan stepped in hoping to take Becky unaware. "Did Ralph put out a contract on me, Becky?"

She looked at Dylan as though he were speaking to her in ancient Hebrew. "I don't know what you mean."

Dylan explained about the shot taken at him in the boat as well as being attacked in his shed by a man with a knife. "Was Ralph behind this?"

Becky shook her head. "No, no, he'd never do something like that!"

"Could some of your friends in the drug trade have a hit out on me?" Noting Becky's reaction, Dylan felt she was truly surprised at his questions.

"They're not my friends," Becky insisted, a pained expression overshadowing her sorrow. "And I've never heard anything about a contract on you. Why would anybody want to kill you, anyway?" She looked down at her hands again. "We thought you were out of the game."

"Something puzzles me about this whole scenario, Becky. Ralph comes from old money. He's got more than he could spend in two lifetimes from what I know of him." Dylan saw the image of Ralph's lean, aristocratic face. "Why would he risk everything to make money from illegal drugs?"

Shaking her head slowly, Becky answered, "He doesn't have the money anymore. Not much, anyway."

"What happened?"

She looked at him again. "He spent most of it getting out of that business with the missing children. You remember the Y.O.U.R. program?"

Dylan thought back seven years to the time of the assassination, Susan's terrible wounds, and Remy, a fifteen-year-old boy trying to be a man in "the hole" in Baton Rouge's downtown jail. "Yeah, I remember it."

"He had to buy off a lot of people, expensive people, to get out of that one." Becky set the glass down on an end table. "It cost him most of his inheritance. Unfortunately, it didn't take away his addiction to politics. And you need a great deal of money to run for governor."

It had never occurred to Dylan that Rayburn would have ambitions that high. After the Y.O.U.R. fiasco of seven years previous, Rayburn had almost vanished as a player in the Baton Rouge political arena. Even his appointment as head of state tourism was an obscure one.

Becky's eyes were shadowed with the beginnings of despair as she gazed at Dylan. "He blamed you for everything, Dylan."

Dylan saw no point in making any comment, feeling that it was best to let Becky release whatever was inside her.

"Once or twice I even tried to make him see that he should just forget about what happened." A puzzled frown crept across Becky's face. "And something else . . . he mentioned several times a tennis match y'all played years ago. He never forgave you for beating him. He seemed to think it humiliated him in front of his wife and his friends."

Becky rubbed her eyes with her fingertips, then stared at the floor, shaking her head slowly. "My whole life's like some kind of soap opera, except that on television something good happens . . . occasionally."

Dylan kept silent as Becky looked at him again, and just for a few moments the old Becky appeared—the girl who had stayed close by him through that long, terrible year after his father's death; the girl who had first taught him about poetry; Becky, who had shared his secret place on the river and talked with him of a time far away when they would be married.

"I'm so sorry, Dylan! I never meant to get you involved in this horrible mess. Things . . . just got out of control. And there was so much money involved—incredible amounts of money. I could have paid off all my debts and had more than enough to last me the rest of my life."

Dylan had let his friendship with Becky cloud his judgment for the last time. "Will you testify against Ralph?"

The words seemed to jerk her out of her dreams of riches. "Do I have to?"

"Things will go much easier for you if you do."

"That phony!" Becky spat the words out bitterly. "Of course, I will."

Seeing the hardness as well as the despair in Becky's eyes, Dylan asked, "Becky, what happened to your faith?"

The anger left her in a flood, leaving her limp and wilted.

"I—I don't know. I've done so many bad things. . . . There's just no way back for me."

Keeping his distance, Dylan thought back to that time weeks earlier when he almost shared his faith with Becky . . . almost. And he felt a terrible sense of loss even as he continued to encourage her. "You know that's not true, Becky. Jesus loves you just as much right now as He did when you were going to church every week and reading your Bible every day."

"I've lived such a terrible life." Tears slipped down her cheeks from her closed eyes.

"Jesus will never turn you away, Becky, no matter what you've done. He said, 'All those that come, I will in no way cast out.' "

Becky nodded slowly, keeping her eyes closed, head bowed. "I'd like to still believe that."

"Just come back to Him with that same faith you had as a girl, and He'll see you through whatever lies ahead of you."

Becky lifted her head, gazing at Dylan with tear-bright eyes. "I . . . I'll try. I have to . . . there's nobody else now."

Dylan stood up then. "It's time to go, Becky."

She gave him one final, pleading look, then stood up. "Will they put handcuffs on me?"

"I can call the police, or I can take you myself."

Becky lifted her chin, as though trying to strengthen her resolve. "I'll go with you."

"I still feel sorry for her." Dylan stared out the window at LSU's ROTC cadets drilling on the open field that ran all the way to Tiger Stadium.

"Sorry for her!" Wes, frying eggs on his two-burner stove, turned a stunned expression on Dylan. "She set you up like a bowling pin, son. She would have ruined your whole life and walked away with the cash."

"She was a good friend, though, when I really needed

one. . . . That's not easy to forget."

"Did she clear you?"

Dylan nodded.

"Well, with what our south-of-the-border gravedigger spilled, that ought to do it. You're out of the woods."

"The DA's already dropped the charges. They're setting up a meeting this afternoon with the DEA and the Federal Prosecutor. She's going to give her full statement then."

Wes dumped his eggs onto a plate, adding grits and four slices of toast. "You want something to eat?"

Dylan shook his head, still gazing at the cadets out on the drill field. All that remained of Vietnam for most of its veterans were the memories and the heartaches and the nightmares. He wondered in what remote or familiar lands these young men would fight their wars for America.

"You don't seem too happy for somebody who just got a twelfth-hour reprieve." Wes sat down at the little table and began to eat his breakfast.

"Guess it hasn't really sunk in yet." Dylan left the window and sat down across from Wes.

"It will. Besides, the best part's still ahead." Wes gave him a sly grin.

"What do you mean?"

Wes chewed a mouthful of eggs and toast, the grin still on his face. "We get to put your ol' tennis buddy in the slammer."

"Ralph?"

"Yep."

"How'd that happen?" Dylan asked, then looked Wes in the eyes and rephrased his question. "How did you manage to make that happen?"

"Who's got a better right to bust the fat cat than the man who broke this whole thing wide open?" He jerked a thumb in Dylan's direction. "Along with his trusty sidekick, o'course."

"We're taking Ralph to jail?"

"They're cuttin' the warrant right now. All we gotta do is

197

drop by the courthouse, pick it up, and Baton Rouge's former golden boy is on the way to the calaboose."

"I don't think Ralph's the first-string quarterback on this team, Wes."

Probably not, but he's at or near the top as far as the ones we can get our hands on right now." Wes stood up, put his dishes in the sink, and slipped on a brown corduroy sport coat, badly in need of cleaning and pressing.

"Why're you getting so dressed up?" Dylan asked, taking in the scuffed boots and faded jeans.

Wes combed his thick hair back from his face with the spread fingers of his left hand. "Gotta look my best for our friend, the consummate politician."

Dylan glanced at Wes's .357 hanging in its holster on the bedpost. "You're not going off half-dressed, are you?"

"No need for artillery now." Lifting the heavy revolver, Wes placed it in the bottom drawer of a battered gray metal desk. "All the hardball players have gone on to greener pastures, except for the ones who were a little slow on the uptake. As soon as we drop our boy Ralph off at the 'Clanging Door Motel,' I'm taking a couple of days off. Me and Chet are goin' fishin'."

"Good for you." Dylan noticed Wes's weathered face brighten considerably as he mentioned his son. "I'll bet he's really looking forward to that."

"Probably not as much as me." Wes grinned and said, "You ready?"

"You won't get into trouble hauling me along?"

"You're reinstated, aren't you?"

"Yep. I talked to Emile on the phone before I left the DA's office."

"Good. We can do everything according to the book, then. Won't have to keep you in the shadows any longer."

Dylan noticed Wes's smile growing wider, the gleam in his eyes. "What's on your devious mind now, Wes?"

He laughed. "Oh, I was just wondering . . . about Ralph." He turned toward Dylan. "Reckon what he'll do first . . . holler for his mama or wet his pants?"

———————

Dylan followed his and Wes's angling shadows up the grand staircase of the state Capitol. Opening one of the heavy bronze and glass doors, they entered the lavishly ornamented Memorial Hall, over one hundred feet long and forty feet wide with a thirty-seven-foot ceiling. Their boots rang with a hollow sound on the marble floor, echoing off the walls as they walked past the bronze relief map of Louisiana and the bullet holes marking the site of Huey Long's assassination.

Wes pushed the button for the elevator. "This is more fun than Mardi Gras! I can't wait to see ol' Ralph's face when I clamp the bracelets on his wrists, right next to them fancy cuff links he always wears."

Dylan gazed at the portraits of Louisiana's governors on the bronze elevator doors. Their cold, dead eyes seemed to reprove him for violating the sanctity of their statehouse. "You think we've got enough on Ralph to make the charges stick?"

Wes gave Dylan his crooked smile. "He's slick all right, but not slick enough to get out of this."

As the elevator doors swished open, they stepped inside and whined upward toward the plush offices filled with the trappings of power and privilege.

"No, I do not have an appointment," Wes bellowed, "but I do have this!" He snatched the warrant from his inside pocket and tossed it onto the receptionist's desk.

The slight blond girl, stylishly dressed and manicured, stared with wide eyes at the rough giant standing before her, then picked up the warrant between thumb and forefinger as though it had begun to contaminate her immaculate and flower-scented waiting room. "Is this for Ralph—I mean, Mr. Rayburn?"

"You can read, can't you, or is just looking good all you need for this job?"

Dylan saw the fear rising in the girl's eyes, her face beginning to flush. "He's harmless," Dylan said, stepping in front of her desk, "just a big ol' teddy bear really." He glanced back at Wes, now glaring at him. "We need to go in and see your boss, and this warrant gives us every right to do that."

"He's not here!" The girl blurted out as though if she spoke quickly enough she would not have to deal with the red-haired ruffian anymore.

"Where is he?"

"You just missed him."

Dylan felt a twinge of uneasiness tickling the back of his neck. "You know where he went?"

The girl shrugged, glancing around Dylan as though reassuring herself that the tall man was being kept in check. "He told me to cancel all his appointments this morning. Then he made several phone calls, cleaned some things out of his office, and left about ten minutes before you got here."

Dylan walked quickly over to the window that looked out onto the Old Arsenal and the eastern gardens. Far below, Ralph, his thick blond hair gleaming in the morning sunshine, carried a heavy cardboard box across the parking lot to his Mercedes convertible, dumped it into the backseat, climbed in, and drove away.

"Whadda you see out there?" Wes called out from the receptionist's desk.

"Ralph. He's leaving." Dylan watched the sleek silver car barreling off down North Fifth, disappearing beneath the overhanging branches of ancient cedars growing along the border of the landscaped Capitol grounds.

"Which way?"

"He's headed downtown."

Wes slammed his boot into the front of the girl's desk, splintering the cherry panel. The receptionist shrieked in terror and ran out of the room into the hallway. Her cries gradually diminished down the stairwell.

"What's she so upset about?" Wes asked innocently. "Desk don't belong to her anyway."

Several people had poked their heads out of doorways and, seeing Wes's scowling face, jerked them back inside.

Dylan headed toward the door. "We'd better get out of here. You can make arrangements to pay for the desk later."

"What's your hurry?" Wes scowled at a man staring in from the hallway. He quickly found business elsewhere. "It's too late to stop Ralph now."

"Maybe so," Dylan responded, pausing at the door, "but I don't feel like explaining all this to Capitol Security right now."

"You're right," Wes agreed. "Just hang on a second." He made a quick call, using the receptionist's telephone, then followed Dylan out the door and down the hall toward the stairs.

Once out of the hall, Dylan's words echoed up and down the stairwell. He gave Wes a troubled look. "Where do you think Ralph's headed?"

Wes favored his bad knee as they descended the stairs. "No way to tell for sure. He's either leaving the state or the country, getting rid of some kind of evidence"—he glanced at Dylan—"or maybe he's already made arrangements to cut his own deal."

"What's your best guess?"

Stopping on a landing, Wes rubbed his bad knee with both hands. "Ralph's not the type to run off and leave the kind of life he was born into here. I doubt he keeps anything around that would tie him directly to the drug traffic." He continued his descent. "But he's probably got the goods on some of the higher-ups our gravedigger friend wouldn't have had any contact with."

"So he's gone to cut a deal?"

"That'd be my guess."

Dylan reached the main floor and stepped out into the hallway. "You don't think the local boys or even the Feds would really go for that, do you?"

Wes walked toward the Memorial Hall, then stopped and peered around the corner.

Taking a look for himself, Dylan saw the receptionist with the damaged desk making frantic motions as she talked with a beefy, gray-haired Capitol policeman, accompanied by several younger officers. After a few instructions from the older man, they all entered the elevator. "You're definitely gonna have to pay for that girl's desk, Wes."

"I reckon so," he agreed reluctantly. "We'd better take the back way out."

"So," Dylan asked, heading toward the back entrance, "you really think they might cut a deal with Ralph?"

"I'd like to think there's more justice in the world than that," Wes said, a shadow of concern flickering in his eyes, "but stranger things have happened. I've seen some real slimeballs let off the hook when they ratted on their buddies." He gazed out at Capitol Lake as they left the building beneath a towering stone portico. "Anyway, let's see if we can head this thing off, if that's what our buddy Ralph has on his mind."

Dylan sat on the concrete steps of the Federal Building watching the afternoon traffic out on Florida Boulevard. The April sunshine felt warm on his face. Leaning back against the bottom railing, he closed his eyes and tried to put the events of the past weeks out of his mind; tried to relax and let the spring weather, the season of light and renewal of life, purge his mind of memories, of darkness, and of the evil that moved in that darkness.

Hearing footsteps behind him, Dylan recognized them as belonging to Wes. He could tell by the leaden step and the slight hesitation as he sat down next to him that his big friend was carrying a burden of bad news.

"Bad news, Dylan."

Dylan opened his eyes slowly, squinting into the slanting sunlight. "Ralph's home free . . . just about."

"How'd you find out?"

"Buddy of mine who works in the Federal Attorney's office. I made a case or two for him over the years, and he gives me the inside scoop now and again.

"They're not going to just turn him loose, are they?"

"Not exactly."

Dylan sat up, placing the palms of his hands flat on the warm concrete. "What does that mean—he gets slapped across the knuckles with a ruler?"

"Two years' probation." Wes sat down across from Dylan, stretching his bad leg out in front of him.

"Two years' probation!" Dylan stood up abruptly, seeing the day through a red haze of anger. "This man's brought misery into hundreds . . . maybe thousands of lives. Who knows how long he's been involved in this. . . ?" He let his words trail off, suddenly feeling old and worn out and useless. The past weeks had taken a heavier toll than he realized, but he gave a silent prayer of thanks that his family was safe and that he could still provide for them. Sitting back down, he continued in a calmer voice. "Ralph's probably made . . . there's no telling how much money he's made in the drug trade. And now he just walks away from it all."

"He gave up some of the big names down south where the drug traffic originates. The Feds can knock a big hole in their business now."

"And Becky. . . ?"

Wes tapped a Camel out of his pack, sticking it in the corner of his mouth. "She's gonna take the fall by herself."

"I thought she had already cut a deal."

Wes shook his head. "Nothing had been finalized." He struck a kitchen match on the concrete railing and lit his cigarette. "And Ralph had all the information she had plus a whole lot more. So they went with him instead."

Dylan watched the sun slide behind a dark cloud in the west, fringing its edges with light. "I believe we've still got the best system in the world," he said solemnly, "but sometimes justice gets lost in the legal shuffle."

"There might be more justice in this than you imagine," Wes said with a wry smile.

"What do you mean?"

Wes held on to his smile. "Ralph refused to enter the witness protection program."

15

THE GOOD-BYE KISS

"Daddy, Daddy, we're home!" Erin, her silky blond hair flying behind her, ran out the door of the shed and down the white shell path leading to the cabin.

"I can see that," Dylan said, leaping down from the gallery and lifting his daughter high in his arms. Balancing her on one hip, he held out his other arm to Susan, who carried hangered clothes over her shoulder and followed her daughter at a more sedate pace.

"We've missed you," Susan said, her clear green eyes glistening with joy. She slid inside Dylan's embrace, kissing him on the mouth.

Pulling back, glancing from his wife to his daughter and back again, he said, "Me too," the only words he seemed able to force past the constriction of his throat.

"Let's go fishin', Daddy!" Erin squirmed to get down. "I'll go get the poles and you can get the motor and—"

"Hold on, short stuff." Dylan grinned and placed Erin on the ground. "We'll visit a little while first. You and Mama can tell me what you did in New Orleans."

"I don't want to talk about that place. I don't like it very much. It's too noisy, and Mama said they won't even let people go hunting in the big park across from Grandma's. There's a lot of squirrels there, too," Erin complained. "Let's go fishin'."

Dylan laughed, slipping his arms around Susan's waist. "You've got a one-track mind, little girl. Just take it easy. We've got years to go fishing." He pulled Susan close and kissed her, then gazed into her eyes, feeling the never-failing comfort that being close to her always brought him. "I missed you."

"You already told her that," Erin insisted, hands on her hips. "It's time to have some fun."

Dylan gazed down at his daughter. "If tenacity means anything in this world, you're all set."

Erin frowned at the word she didn't understand, then gave it her own meaning. "I'm all set to go fishin'."

"Are you hungry?"

Erin thought about that for a few seconds. "Kinda."

"Good. I fixed some lunch."

Susan gave her husband an incredulous look. "*You* . . . cooked lunch?"

"*Fixed*," Dylan corrected her. "I didn't say anything about cooking."

"Does that mean you spooned some ice cream into a bowl or took the wrapper off a Tootsie Roll?"

Erin looked at her daddy and giggled. "Mama says you couldn't make toast without a recipe."

Susan waggled her finger at Erin in mock scolding. "You're not supposed to give away our secrets, young lady. Now let's go see this sumptuous meal your daddy's . . . *fixed* for us." She gave Dylan a dubious look. "Uh . . . what's on the menu, Chef St. John?"

"Tuna fish sandwiches, potato chips, and pickles," Dylan said proudly.

"That he can handle," Susan said, nodding toward her daughter. "Your daddy can open a can with the best of them."

Dylan lay in bed, Susan nestled in the crook of his arm, her head in the hollow of his shoulder. The night wind blew the long sheer curtains into the room. Dylan felt it cool and soft across his face and his bare chest.

" 'Blessed is he whose transgression is forgiven . . .' " Susan's breath was warm against his skin.

"I'm supposed to—"

" '. . . whose sin is covered,' " Susan continued, paying no attention to her husband's protest.

"Psalms, it's from the psalms."

" 'Blessed is the man unto whom the Lord imputeth not iniquity . . .' "

"Give me a chance, will you?" Dylan smiled as he recalled the times when he had done the same thing to Susan, realizing that he was getting his just due.

" '. . . and in whose spirit there is no guile.' "

"Hold on now, I'm about to—"

"Psalm thirty-two, verses one and two," Susan said, holding back her laughter.

Dylan propped himself on one elbow, gazing down at her. "Is that any way for a Christian woman to treat her husband? You didn't give me a chance to think."

"The flesh just rose up in me, sweetheart." Susan grinned. "I couldn't help myself." She poked Dylan in the stomach with a slim finger. "But I won, didn't I?"

"I knew what it was all along."

Susan sat up. "You did not!"

"Sure I did," Dylan insisted, pushing his tousled hair back from his face. "I have to let you win once in a while or you'll start whining and quit playing the game."

Refusing to be drawn in, Susan merely smiled at her husband, content in her victory. She fluffed up her pillow, placed it against the headboard, and settled back against it. "I think that's what I like about you most."

"You mean that I let you win sometimes?"

But Susan had already put the game behind her. "A man

'in whose spirit there is no guile.' " The light in her eyes softened as she looked at Dylan. "When we were going through all those hard times, even then I knew you'd tell me the truth." She shrugged. "Of course, some of it wasn't very pretty, but you just seemed incapable of sustaining a lie, even if you started out to tell one."

The breeze through the window ruffled Susan's hair, gleaming in the faint moonlight. "I remember one time you told me you were going somewhere . . . I don't even remember the circumstances now . . . but I remember what happened. Two minutes later you came back into the house looking like a little boy with a bad report card. It wasn't about anything important either," she continued, "but it wasn't the truth. It was almost like the lie was poisoning you, and you had to spew it out of your life."

"You can give credit to Noah St. John for that." Dylan smiled at the thought of his father and the one time he had caught Dylan in a lie, though he hadn't found it humorous at all back then. "He wouldn't abide a liar in his home."

"I'm glad he was so narrow-minded."

"Daddy . . ."

Dylan looked at the slight and shadowy figure standing in the hallway just outside their door. "Yes, Erin. I set the alarm clock for five in the morning. The fish won't even be awake when we get there."

"I wanted to be sure."

"It's way past your bedtime, sweetheart," Susan said with a yawn.

"I know. I just . . . I just . . ."

Dylan called back his daughter's words of an hour before, when he had prayed with her at her bedside before tucking her in for the night. She had said, "I didn't like it when you wasn't with Mama and me. It made me hurt"—she had placed her hand on her chest then—"in here."

"Come on, you little night owl," Dylan said, holding his

arms out toward his daughter. "Hop in with us."

Erin scurried across the hardwood floor, leaping onto Dylan's chest. "I like this big bed!" She rolled between Dylan and Susan, finding a place for her head on Susan's pillow. "I know, let's sing. 'Jesus loves me, this I know.'" She sang with childlike vigor, then looked at her parents. "Sing with me."

They sang along with her, and then sang another of her Sunday school songs, and then another. Much later, Dylan lifted his sleeping daughter in his arms and carried her back to her bedroom. Placing her on the sun-fresh sheet and pulling the covers up, he kissed her on the cheek. Then he knelt at her bedside, holding one of her small hands. His heart seemed to overflow as he prayed. "Father, thank you for this precious child and for the joy she's brought to our family. Thank you for Susan. I never could have made it all these years without her. Thank you for . . ."

"Whadda you got there?" Wes, toweling his hair dry and wearing only a pair of navy dress slacks, opened the door, motioning for Dylan to come in.

"Home cookin'," Dylan said, carrying the brown paper grocery bag over to Wes's dinette.

Wes headed down the short hall toward the bathroom as he spoke. "I never knew you to do any home cookin'. What's the occasion?"

"The cooking's not mine," Dylan replied, taking a pot and several bowls out of the bag and placing them on the table, "and the occasion is that Susan wanted to thank you for looking out for her incompetent and gullible husband."

"Gullible is the word, all right." Wes opened the sliding door to his closet across the hall from the bathroom, selected a white dress shirt with a button-down collar, and slipped it on. He walked over to the table and began examining the feast Dylan was laying out. "After all this time working with street thugs and deviants and other assorted felons, you still believe most people are gonna tell you the truth, and that deep down they're just like you are. That just ain't the way the world is, son."

"No, I don't."

"You don't what?"

"Whatever it was you said I do," Dylan replied. "What are you talking about anyway?"

"Just serve the food." Wes hooked a chair out with his foot and sat down. "I can see you're not mature enough to deal with profound thoughts and cosmic realities."

Dylan stopped spooning fluffy white rice into a large bowl. "I *could* take all this food back home, though."

"Like I was saying"—Wes grinned—"you're just about the most intellectual person I know. Now, what did your lovely wife fix for a lonely bachelor?"

"Shrimp gumbo."

"Hot dog! She knows that's my favorite."

"What's the occasion?"

"For what?"

"Dress slacks and a white shirt. You must have a date with somebody real special."

Wes mumbled, keeping his eyes on the food. "My wife."

"Vicki. You're going out with Vicki?"

Wes took a deep breath, then looked Dylan in the eyes. "Yep. I been off the pills for months now. We've been talking and . . . well, one thing led to another, and we decided to give our marriage another chance."

"That's great! I'll bet Chet's tickled about that."

Wes nodded, giving Dylan his crooked half-smile. "I figured if you could change enough to be a decent husband and father, there might be hope for me, too."

Dylan served the steaming gumbo, rich and spicy and full of succulent fresh shrimp, over the rice, then unwrapped the French bread, basted with garlic butter, from its aluminum foil and placed it on a plate. "Guess that's it. Dig in."

Wes had already begun to eat. He unscrewed the top of a quart Mason jar Dylan had taken from the bag and took a long swallow of sweetened iced tea.

"Can I get you a glass for that?"

"What for? I'm gonna drink it all anyway."

"Something just occurred to me."

"Oh yeah? What's that?"

"Did you ever pay for that desk you demolished over at the Capitol?"

"You would think of that," Wes moaned. "What're you trying to do, give me indigestion?"

"I just wondered what happened, that's all."

Wes spoke through a mouthful of gumbo and rice. "Not only did I have to pay for the desk, I had to go over there and apologize to that panicky girl. You shoulda seen that act. You'd have thought she was the Queen Mother and I'd been caught poaching deer from the Royal Forest."

"Could have been worse," Dylan observed. "They could have charged you with criminal damage to property."

"Someone was kind enough to point that out to me. In fact, that was the reason I went."

Dylan watched his big friend devouring his meal. "I guess I can safely tell Susan you enjoyed her cooking."

Wes nodded, tearing off a hunk of bread with his teeth, chewing it with relish. Swallowing, he said, "I been watching you these past few weeks."

Dylan had no idea what Wes's intentions were but decided to keep quiet . . . and not drop his guard.

"Something's really changed you since we used to work to-gether in the parole department." Wes chewed thoughtfully, his eyes on Dylan. "I know part of it must be having Susan for a wife, and then . . . well, you're a father now, and that usually makes a big difference in a man's life."

"Right on both counts."

"All the things you went through: somebody trying to stop your clock; criminal charges hanging over your head; losing your job; having to send your family out of town; betrayed by an old friend you'd known since y'all were kids together." Wes gazed intently into Dylan's eyes. "I'd probably have put a gun barrel in my mouth if I'd been in your place. What's your secret?"

Dylan spoke directly from the heart. "A few years back I came to believe that Jesus Christ is exactly who He says He is."

Wes's eyes narrowed in a skeptical look. "Oh yeah? How'd that happen?"

"When Erin was in the hospital and we didn't think she was gonna make it . . . and there was nothing we could do to help her." Dylan saw Erin again in her incubator; heard the hum and rush of air, the bleeps of the monitoring equipment, all working to keep life in the tiny, fragile body. "I didn't know what else to do, so I just cried out to God for help."

Wes, a spoonful of gumbo halfway to his mouth, stared transfixed at Dylan.

"I remembered a verse my grandmother used to read to me. Jesus said, 'Come unto me, all ye that labour and are heavy laden, and I will give you rest.' " Dylan took a deep breath. "That night in the hospital I gave my life to Jesus and . . . things were different. I just had a kind of peace about things after that." He looked at Wes staring back intently at him. "I know this sounds real strange, Wes, but it's what happened to me."

Wes ate another spoon of gumbo, chewing thoughtfully. "I used to go to church when I was a kid. Even tried reading the Bible a time or two. Never made much sense to me."

"Some of it's pretty simple."

"Like what?"

"Romans 10:9. It says—"

"Hold on now," Wes cut him off. "I don't want to hear no sermon at the dinner table."

Dylan laughed. "All right, but do one thing for me."

212

Wes laid his spoon on the edge of the bowl. The skeptical look was back.

"Read that verse for me."

Wes grinned. "One verse? I can do that much."

"Then read the book of John."

"You're pressing your luck, son."

Dylan stared at the bowl. "You like that gumbo?"

Wes shook his head sadly. "You oughta be ashamed of yourself, threatening to cut off my gumbo supply."

"I'm mortified."

"Awright, I'll read John's book." Wes held up both hands, palms outward. "Now let me enjoy my dinner, will you? You're gonna give me heartburn."

Dylan smiled at his old friend. "God says if you seek Him with all your heart, you'll find Him. You might be heading down that road right now."

"Don't count on me teaching Sunday school classes no time soon." Wes dug into the gumbo. "Man, this is good stuff! You be sure to tell Susan how much I appreciate her cooking for me."

———

Sweat poured in rivulets down Dylan's face, chest, and back. The afternoon sunlight felt like the heat near an open flame as he pushed the lawnmower through the thick grass on the north end of the cabin away from the shed and the boat dock. His cutoff Levi's were soaked and his bare feet squished in his tennis shoes with each step he took.

Dylan's eyes followed the fresh-cut swath through the grass as he plodded along behind the mower. Making a turn toward the road, he glanced up and saw a tall man standing in the shade of a sweet gum tree. His black hair was long and he wore cowboy boots, jeans, and a black twill shirt with the sleeves cut off, revealing tanned muscular arms. A western style .44 revolver in a hand-tooled leather holster hung on his lean hips.

What're you doing here? I've already killed you, Dylan thought absurdly.

The man pulled the revolver, began twirling it, and stepped out into the bright sunshine, walking toward Dylan with slow, measured steps.

Dylan saw again the scene at the bayou's edge, the acetylene flash of the revolver; heard the bullet whine past his ear; felt the kick of his Colt as he fired four shots at the tall, dark-haired man in the tan trench coat.

The man with the pistol gave Dylan a cold grin. "I see you don't have a shovel with you this time."

That night in the shed—the shadowy figure and the knife. "Who are you?"

"The Grim Reaper." The man held the revolver steady now, its black muzzle pointed at Dylan's chest.

Dylan's mind raced. He glanced about for some kind of weapon or an escape route, but he was standing in the open in bright daylight, facing an armed man ten feet away. He barely heard the little three-horse Briggs and Stratton engine rattling and growling as though eager to finish its task, then looked into the dark, cold depths of the gunman's eyes. "What do you want?"

The man pulled two six-foot lengths of yellow nylon cord from his back pocket, tossing them at Dylan's feet. "I want you to sit down . . . now!"

Dylan sat down on the mowed grass, feeling it stick to the underside of his legs.

"Now," the man began, his lips thin and white against his dark face, "tie your ankles together, and then tie your right hand against your waist."

Dylan looped one of the cords around his ankles, trying to leave a little slack for movement.

"Tighter!" the man shouted. "You try to mess with me, I'll blow your kneecaps off right now."

His breath ragged in his throat from the heat, physical exertion, and a growing fear of what this man was about to do to him, Dylan pulled the cord tight, then looped the other around his wrist, passed it around his waist and secured it tightly.

"Flat on your back!"

Dylan stared at the pistol, rock steady in the big man's hand. He lay back.

"Now bend your knees."

As soon as Dylan complied with the man's demand, he quickly knelt, grabbed Dylan's free wrist, and bound it to the cord that secured his ankles.

Dylan now lay on his back, his left side slightly raised by the left arm extended and bound to his ankles. He watched the man's lips draw back over his white teeth in what appeared to be an attempt at a smile.

"Now for the fun." Suddenly the man knelt down, straddling Dylan's chest, his knees pressing heavily against the already bound arms. Then in a slow and deliberate motion, he pulled from his shirt pocket a clear plastic bag with a white drawstring at one end.

Dylan felt a cold terror fill his mind, blocking out everything but the will to survive. He struggled, but the big man's weight pressing against his chest made movement impossible. He gasped for breath as the air was slowly pushed out of his lungs.

In a sudden, precise movement, the man slipped the bag over Dylan's head and drew the strings taut around his neck, cutting off his air supply.

Dylan saw the man's black eyes, cold and remote, staring down at him. The sound of the lawnmower called him back to the everyday things of life, but that life was over since this man had stepped out of the black shade. Dylan stared up at the blue sky, towering toward infinity. He gasped open-mouthed for air that no longer existed.

Then, as in a dream, he saw Susan through the cloudy plastic. She stood behind the man, a small wooden baseball bat clutched in both hands. Dylan remembered buying it for Erin at the Woolworth's store in Evangeline. *She's holding it at the bottom of the handle. She'll get plenty of power that way.*

And she did. Dylan saw Susan draw her arms back as though she had just stepped up to the batter's box, then swing with all her strength. The bat slammed against the man's temple with a sickening thud. His head jerked to one side, and the cold light in his eyes flickered and winked out. Slowly, he collapsed on the freshly cut grass.

"Becky told me her husband had a brother," Dylan said, holding the door open for Susan as they left the sheriff's office. "She didn't tell me he was a twin brother and a homicidal maniac bent on revenge."

"Maybe she didn't know." Susan took Dylan's arm as they walked across the courthouse grounds. Wearing white cotton slacks and a pale blue blouse, she looked cool and serene in the shade of the old live oaks.

"Maybe not," Dylan agreed. His near brush with death had left him weak and still a little disoriented. He felt almost as though he were a stranger in this world of flesh-and-blood people.

"You hungry?"

Dylan shook his head, then looked down at his clothes. He had slipped on a threadbare white T-shirt with *LSU Tennis* printed in purple letters across the front and still wore his cutoff Levi's and tennis shoes. "I'm not exactly dressed for going to a restaurant, anyway."

"Could we sit down for a minute?"

Dylan felt the pressure of Susan's hand on his arm. Her face looked pale and drawn. "Are you all right?"

"No." Susan's words were barely a whisper.

Leading her over to a stone bench, Dylan sat down next to

her. "Maybe I should take you to the hospital?"

"No, no, I'll be all right," Susan protested mildly. "I just felt a little weak, that's all."

Dylan took his wife's hand. It felt remarkably cool and dry in the humid warmth of the late afternoon. "Are you sure you're all right, Susan?"

"No . . . I'm not." She gave him a weak smile, then leaned over and kissed him on the cheek. "But I will be."

They sat together in the shelter of the old trees while Evangeline went about its business. A few shoppers strolled the sidewalks, peering into the store windows. Some even went inside and made purchases. People hurried or strolled up and down the wide stone steps of the courthouse, its huge white columns gleaming in the amber slanting light.

"Susan . . ."

"Yes." She spoke in a hushed tone, leaning her head on Dylan's shoulder, her eyes closed.

"Why did you come back? You were supposed to be on the way to Emmaline's to pick up Erin."

"You'll think I'm silly."

"No, I won't."

Susan sat up, her clear green eyes filling with a soft light. "I forgot to kiss you good-bye."

"You did? I mean I'm glad you did, otherwise . . ."

"I just got to thinking after I'd driven a few miles that something could happen to you and I'd missed that last chance to kiss you." Susan gave him a sleepy smile. "It sounds kind of silly, even to me."

"I like silly, then. Silly kept me breathing. I think it's something we're going to hang on to." Dylan gazed thoughtfully at a young couple going into Paw Paw's Cafe across the street. "He must have been hiding somewhere nearby, waiting for you to leave. I expect they'll find his car within a half mile of our place."

A shadow of concern crossed Susan's face. "Do you . . . you

don't think he'll ever try anything again?"

"Not likely. Emile ran a check on him. He was in jail in South Dakota waiting for sentencing on a second-degree murder conviction when he escaped. If he ever gets out of prison up there, they'll notify us and he'll be transported here to face attempted murder charges. No, I don't think we'll ever see him again."

Susan's face brightened as the tension seemed to flow out of her body. "You ready to go pick up Erin? I'm sure she must have Emma worn to a frazzle."

"Yep." Dylan nodded and took Susan's hand as she stood up. "There might even be enough daylight left to finish mowing the grass."

"I know you're thrilled about that," Susan said, knowing how Dylan detested grass cutting.

"Not especially, but like my ol' DI used to tell us in boot camp, 'It must be did.' "

Susan smiled and slipped inside his arms, pressing closely against him, her face against his chest.

Dylan felt her trembling slightly. He caressed the back of her neck, kissed her forehead. "I'm kind of dirty for romance, Mrs. St. John."

"Hush," Susan whispered. "Just hold me for a minute. I'm getting better."

EPILOGUE

Dylan pulled into the shed, cut the engine, and listened to the drumming of rain on the tin roof. Then it suddenly came down harder, changing the sound to a dull roar. "She's sound asleep," he said, glancing at the backseat where Erin lay curled up, her head pillowed on his folded black suit coat.

"It's been a long, hard day for a little girl." Susan's face softened in a serene smile the way it always did when she looked at her sleeping daughter.

"I'll take her," Dylan said, opening the door and lifting her limp form in his arms.

Susan placed Dylan's coat over Erin and got out on the other side of the car. Then she opened the umbrella and held it over the three of them as they walked down the shell path, glistening white in the lead-colored light, to the cabin. When they reached the door, she said, "Here, I'll take her on in and put her to bed. I have an idea you'd like to watch the rain for a while."

Dylan nodded, kissed his daughter on the forehead, and gave her to Susan. Then, putting his coat back on, he walked across the gallery to the porch swing, sat down, and slipped out of his shoes. Unloosening his tie, he lifted his legs onto the swing and leaned back against the armrest.

The rain pounded the flowerbeds at the edge of the gallery, clattered on the broad, glistening leaves of the banana plant, and made a flat, splattering sound out on the planking of the dock. At the bayou's edge, cattails wobbled in the wind.

Dylan thought of another time of rain, his first day of school. Sitting on the back porch of his house in Algiers, he had touched the bruise on his cheek where an older boy had pushed him down on the hardpan of the schoolyard, and he could almost hear the taunts of the other children. The bruise on his heart showed not at all but went much deeper.

His mother had come out onto the porch, bringing him a saucer of homemade cookies and a frothy, cold glass of milk. Time had taken away her words, but he did remember how good the cookies were and the sound of his mother's soothing voice and how much better he had felt afterward.

"It's kind of chilly out here," Susan said, walking over to the swing. She had changed into a pair of Dylan's tennis socks, gray sweat pants, and a white cotton sweater. Sitting down on the opposite end facing Dylan, she stretched her legs out, her feet in Dylan's lap.

Still lost in his memories, Dylan began rubbing Susan's perpetually cold feet. A gust of wind blew a sudden cold mist underneath the gallery roof. "You want to go inside?"

"No. It's too pretty to leave." Susan gazed out at the rain-swept bayou and the limbs of the weeping willow bending in the wind. Then she looked thoughtfully at Dylan. "You want to read the letter now?"

Dylan nodded and pulled a white envelope from his inside coat pocket. On the front his mother had written *Dylan* in her fine flowing script. Opening the envelope, he took out a sheet of powder blue stationery, carefully unfolded it, and read:

My dearest son,

When you read this, I will be with my Lord. An angel visited me several days ago. After he left, I decided to write you this letter. I know it sounds strange about the angel, but it was a marvelous experience . . . and it was real, more real to me than the things of this world.

Noah was such a good husband—the love of my life. When he left, he took my heart with him, but we are together now and we'll